TO MARRY A MARCHIONESS

Lords of London, Book 6

TAMARA GILL

To Marry a Marchioness
Lords of London, Book 6
Copyright © 2019 by Tamara Gill
Cover Art by Wicked Smart Designs
Editor Authors Designs
Editor Free Bird Editing
All rights reserved.

ISBN 10: 0-6484133-7-3
ISBN 13: 978-0-6484133-7-0

DEDICATION

To my wonderful readers. Thank you for walking this journey with me.

CHAPTER 1

L ady Henrietta Nicholson, Marchioness of Zetland, sat before her bedroom dressing table and stared at her reflection. Her eyes were bloodshot and puffy, the tip of her nose was red, and her hair had somehow refused to be appropriate on this sombre day and stay confined under her hairpins.

Behind her, her maid bustled about the room, making her bed that now looked too large, empty, and cold, much like her life as she would know it from this day forward. Her mother, the Duchess of Athelby, was downstairs and not willing to leave Henrietta alone in this large estate that was now hers. The property had not been entailed, and she was free to live out the rest of her days in Surrey if she wished. How wonderful that idea sounded. Having laid her husband to rest in the cold, damp soil not an hour before, Henrietta needed something to look forward to.

She swiped at the tears that fell down her cheeks. How could this be her life? They had only been married twelve short months, it wasn't possible for Walter to be gone. His sickness had been so fast, a trifling cold that had settled in his lungs and then would not budge. No matter what they tried, or how many doctors they'd seen on Harley Street, his cough and his breathing steadily became worse until he passed in his sleep.

Henrietta thought back to the day she'd come upon him in their bedroom fighting for breath, and she'd known with sickening dread that he wasn't long for this earth. That the ailment that had wrought carnage on his body would win the war. Wanting to be strong for him, she'd not broken down until alone, and she had remained steadfast in her ability to remain calm in his presence, to try and keep him cheerful, when all the while her heart was crumbling in her chest knowing that he was slipping away. That she was going to lose him.

If only it had been a peaceful passing. His chest had rattled fiercely during the last hours and Henrietta had prepared herself as best she could. And now the worst was here and she was alone. The man she loved was no longer of this realm, and no matter how much her mother tried to comfort her, it was not her that Henrietta wanted at her side.

She sniffed and started to pull out what few pins she had left in her hair, placing them on the shallow crystal dish on her dressing table. Her mother wanted her to return to town with her, but Henrietta would stay in Surrey. This was her home now, the place she'd been happiest, and she wasn't willing to leave it only to be bombarded in town with pitying looks from friends and acquaintances, constant attempts to comfort and relay their sadness regarding her loss.

Her closest friends meant well, and she was thankful they'd come to Surrey to pay their last respects, but the social whirl of London no longer drew her like it once had. Over the past year she'd become accustomed to country living, to running a large home of her own. The frivolities of London life seemed empty and silly now. The gossip and scandal. As much as she'd miss her friends, on the morrow she would bid them goodbye and selfishly be thankful for it.

Should she return to town the ton would expect her to marry again, and she would never do such a thing. She would not cheat another husband out of what they rightfully needed upon marriage—children. No, she was a widow. She would become a matron of the ton—if a very young one—when she eventually did return, and that would be her life.

A light knock sounded on the door and her maid opened it, revealing her mother. Even in middle age, the Duchess of Athelby was a beautiful woman. Many said that Henrietta took after her mama more than her dearest papa, but she'd always liked to think that she and her twin brother Henry took after them both.

"Are you alright, dearest? I thought I'd sleep in here with you this evening."

Henrietta smiled, taking in her mother in her nightgown and bare feet. Even if she'd wanted to be alone this evening, it was pointless to argue with her mama. If she thought she needed to stay, to give comfort—even if that comfort was without words—there was little Henrietta could say to persuade her otherwise.

"You may stay, Mama. I do not mind."

Her mother dismissed the maid and climbed up into the bed, arranging some pillows so she could sit upright.

"Have you given any thought to returning to London with me next week? Or perhaps even Ruxton estate? Your father thought it may be good for you to close up Kewell Hall and come home for a while. Henry too. We discussed it this evening after you retired."

Did they just. Henrietta pushed away the flicker of annoyance that her family was arranging her, for they really only meant well. Today had been hard on them too, she reminded herself. They had loved Walter—there were few who did not—and they would miss him. "I have given it some thought," she said, standing and walking over to the bed, playing idly with the linens. "But I'm going to remain here, Mama. I promise I shall be fine," she continued when her mother looked at her with something akin to horror. "I will not do anything silly, but I want...no, I need, time to be alone. To come to terms with the fact that I'm a widow and Walter is gone. You understand, do you not? I shall return to town after my year of mourning, but until then, I want to be here. Near my horses, our pets, our garden and home. I just need to heal before I start running to where I'll never face the truth of my life." The truth being now that Walter was gone, she would be alone. Forever.

Her mama nodded, her eyes hooded with sadness. "You've been so strong throughout this whole ordeal, my dear. It is acceptable to break when we lose someone we love. Fortunately, you've never lost a loved one before, so I worry that you're bottling your emotions up."

Henrietta swallowed the lump in her throat. She had been strong, and now that she no longer needed to be, all she wished was to be alone. To crumble and break by herself so she may put the pieces of her life back together. She'd never been an impractical woman, but something told her she'd be anything but her usual self in the next few months.

"I love you so much, darling," her mama said. "If I could take away this pain, if I could turn back the clock and give you Walter back, I would in a heartbeat. I'll worry for you if you stay here. Maybe I could delay my departure. I'm sure your papa will not mind in the least."

Henrietta climbed up into bed beside her mama, lying down and cuddling into her arms. "I want you to go with Papa. I'm sad, and I shall cry just as we are now, but I shall be fine. In time. I promise I shall write to you every week, but I need to be on my own at present. I promise all will be well again." Henrietta hoped that was true. The estate and the people who depended on its success were relying on her to make it so. The new marquess would take care of Walter's other properties, but Kewell Hall was her responsibility and she would not fail these people. She would give herself a month at best to grieve and then she would have to rally and push herself into everyday duties. It was what Walter would want her to do. He loved her so very much that he'd never want her to wallow in unhappiness forever.

Her mother ran a hand through her hair, and Henrietta heard her sigh of defeat. "Very well, we shall return to town next week as planned. But I will visit every month or so. Surrey is not so far away, and for my own sanity you shall allow me to. I will never rest easy if I do not know that my baby girl is well."

Henrietta smiled, hugging her mama tighter. "I love you."

Her mother reached down and kissed her hair. "I love you too, my darling girl. And I promise you, your grief will lessen in time, and you'll find that life will carry on, even if you do not want it to. But it will, and when you're ready, you'll love again. You're too young, with too much of a beautiful soul, to be a widow forever."

The idea made Henrietta shudder. The thought of marrying again, of being intimate, of sharing any kind of life with someone who was not Walter was too abhorrent to imagine. She would never marry again, for the love of her life was gone, and such a love only came around once. No one was ever lucky enough to find two great loves in their life. Her mother ought to know very well how true that was, since Henrietta's father the Duke of Athelby was her mama's second marriage after her disastrous first one.

"You know as well as anyone that marriage will not happen again for me, Mama. I cannot marry a man knowing that I'm unable to bear children."

"The doctors could be wrong, dearest," her mother said.

Even to Henrietta her mother's tone held a sliver of despair. "A year of marriage and not one child, Mama. I think in my case they were correct, and I need to accept my fate. I will never be a mother." Not wanting to give her any more reason to worry, or to discuss the matter any further, she yawned, tiredness swamping her. "I need to sleep now, Mama."

"Very well." Her mother settled beside her. "Goodnight, darling."

"Goodnight, Mama." At least in sleep she might be oblivious to the pain that ricocheted through her with every breath. A pain that only sleep would relieve. A pain that she doubted would ever go away.

MARCUS DUNCAN SAT before the roaring fire in his library and read the missive notifying him that his distant cousin, the Marquess of Zetland, had passed away suddenly and unexpectedly from some sort of lung ailment.

He shook his head at the windfall that couldn't have happened at a better time. The knowledge that the marquessate was now his, along with all the properties that came with it, filled him with joy, as well as with despair for the late marquess's family. No one wished to come into lands, money, and a title in such a way, and he would write to them and support them in their grief.

It would also mean, ultimately, that he would have to travel from Scotland to England—leave his beloved son and homeland and deal with the legalities of the situation. Marcus looked down at Arthur, who was sitting with his nurse, playing with a wooden horse. Although his boy would not inherit the marquessate, or the unentailed lands and properties, his future would be more secure. The income Marcus would draw from the estates would help rebuild and repair his own here in Scotland, giving his son a solid footing for the future.

Guilt pricked his soul that he'd not been able to give that solid footing himself just by siring the boy. When one was born out of wedlock, the stigma followed like the waft of cow dung. But now that there was the possibility of fortune favouring them, well, that could change things a little for his lad, and that alone made him thankful.

He skimmed through the legal document that accompanied the letter from his solicitor in Edinburgh stating that his cousin's widow, the marchioness, had remained at Kewell Hall, but that there was some sort of trouble regarding who owned this unentailed estate and that further correspondence would be forthcoming.

Marcus supposed he would have to look over the estates, ensure all were in working order, and lease them out before he headed back to Scotland. His solicitor mentioned the possibility of leasing out the London townhouse as well, an income source that was timely due to the repairs required at his castle. Not that he had wished death upon his cousin, never that, but he would have to think in terms of his own financial responsibilities now that the marquisate was his.

Once the weather was better he would travel south,

maybe in a month or two, but first he would have to go to Edinburgh to sign off on the inheritance and officially become the new Marquess of Zetland.

The name Zetland didn't roll off the tongue as well as Duncan did, but he'd never thought to inherit the title. His poor cousin. Dying at such a young age, and without heirs, must be a terrible blow to the family, and as much as they would hate anyone distant inheriting the seat, Marcus would do all that he could to help them with their grief. He may be a hard man, but he was not unkind.

He stood and went over to his desk, sitting down behind the four feet of mahogany. Sliding a piece of parchment closer, he scribbled a note to his solicitor that he would attend his office next week. As for when he'd leave for England, well, he would think of that later. With his own estate to take care of here in Scotland, and preparing for planting, he didn't have time right now to oversee the estates in England. His son needed him, and the windfall of inheriting the marquessate would give him some extra funds so work could commence on the east wing of his home. He couldn't very well leave now that he had an opportunity to complete all of the building repairs he'd longed to do. There were also numerous crofters homes that needed new roofing prior to winter, and other repairs that had only been temporary until his fortunes turned.

He would ensure the steward overseeing the marquess's homes started proceedings to lease out the properties to anyone who was interested, and have his solicitor forward any correspondence to him here. For the time being, this would be where he'd deal with any business at hand.

CHAPTER 2

One year later

The carriage ride from Scotland was long—too long to be doing again anytime soon. Marcus jumped down when the vehicle stopped before the last estate, the very one where the widow marchioness resided. Although since the property was his, he really had thought she would have vacated the home by now.

He glanced up at the Georgian sandstone structure, noting the large rectangular windows that glistened in the afternoon sun. The grounds were well kept and resembled a parkland more than the manicured estates the English were so very fond of. He liked this design much better—it was more natural, more to his tastes.

He stretched and adjusted his cravat, checking his attire would be suitable to meet his cousin's widow. He doubted she'd be very pleased to see him, since he would be broaching the subject of why she was still here and not living somewhere else.

The front door opened, and a footman in red livery stepped out, bowing to him. "May I help you, my lord?"

Marcus walked up to the young man. His height and the fact he was quite broad did often bring out the fear of God on people's faces, and the young servant was no different. The lad peered up at him as if he were facing his demise.

"Please tell Lady Zetland that the Marquess of Zetland is here to see her."

The footman's eyes widened, but he nodded. "Follow me if you please, and I shall notify her ladyship of your arrival."

Marcus followed the lad indoors. The home was clean, well kept, and didn't appear in need of any repairs. Over the last few months he'd ensured the other two properties he'd inherited in England were let to good and upstanding families, and he was happy to do the same with this estate. Once Lady Zetland vacated of course, unless she wished to take up the lease, and then he would be more than pleased to leave her well alone so he could return to Scotland.

"This way, my lord. Lady Zetland is in the library."

Marcus followed the lad into a room that was floor to ceiling full of books. A roaring fire burned in the grate, and the deep green and red leather furniture gave the room a masculine feel. He admired it, and should he wish to keep the home, he could admit to feeling quite content in a room like this. The layout was very similar to how he had his own library set up in Scotland.

The footman gestured for him to enter. He glanced across the room and his steps faltered before he righted himself and continued on to meet her ladyship. "In ainm Dé," he muttered in Gaelic. He'd not expected that! "Lady Zetland, I'm sorry we're to meet under such sad circumstances. May I offer you my condolences."

She was standing behind the desk. Her morning gown of the lightest blue reminded him of Scottish skies in summer. Her hair was half up, the remainder of her coppery brown locks falling about her shoulders, and his fingers itched to see if it was as soft as it looked.

She held out her delicate hand and he took it, bowing over it. "Please, have a seat, Lord Zetland. I wish we were meeting under different circumstances as well, but alas, life is not always fair."

That he could agree with. Taking a seat, he took in the room some more, anything but to stare at a woman he'd not thought would be as attractive as she was. With her large, luminous eyes and unblemished skin, she was a perfect English rose. He could all too well feel sorry for his cousin if he died leaving such a woman behind to go on with her life. It would be enough to kill him all over again at the thought of someone else marrying his widow.

"You requested a meeting today, although I'm not sure as to why," she said. "Was there something you wished to discuss with me regarding the estates you've taken over? I worked with Walter quite extensively prior to his death, so I do have some idea of how things work."

Marcus shook his head, clearing his throat. "Oh no, all the estates have been leased and taken care of. I'm Scottish, if ye hadn't already guessed from my accent, and will be returning north within the week. But I do have a query about this home."

She frowned, and even the little line between her brows didn't detract from her prettiness. No woman should be so discombobulating, but it would seem the marchioness had him at a loss and certainly was wreaking havoc on the speed his blood was pumping about his body.

"What do you wish to know?" she asked, her large blue eyes clear and intelligent.

Did she really not know? "Well, as to that, and I don't mean to be unfeeling, but this was also part of my inheritance upon taking up the title."

Her ladyship paled, and Marcus fought not to expire of shame at having to bring up the matter. He would have a very stern word with his lawyer when he saw him again.

"Forgive me, Lady Zetland, I thought you knew. I gave you time, over twelve months to be exact, as I thought you needed the time to heal, to mourn. But when my solicitor mentioned you were still residing here upon my travelling to England, I wanted to see for myself if there was a reason as to why you've not moved. Did you not know?" he asked, hating that she looked like she'd seen a ghost.

"But this house is mine. Walter left it to me upon his death." She moved over to a large cupboard behind her and pulled one of the drawers open, before clasping a rolled piece of parchment. "Here, this is the document."

She handed it to Marcus and he opened it and straight away saw the glaring error. "He has not signed it, Lady Zetland. The decree certainly states that the home ought to go to you, but it's not signed." At her dejected look, he inwardly cringed. He was never one to take what did not belong to him, and should he not need the funds for his lad he would gladly walk away from the estate. As his financial situation now stood, that option was not open to him.

"Surely not!" she took the document from him and scanned it before slumping back into her chair. "Oh my, this is dreadful. I don't understand. I don't understand why my lawyer did not pick up on this."

Neither did Marcus, and he hated to be the bearer of bad news. But the house was his, and not entailed, so he could do what he wanted with it. He didn't want to push Lady Zetland out, so maybe there was something he could do for her in return, since she was innocent in this mess.

"Let me seek information regarding the legalities of the problem we now face. Mayhap there is another document that is signed that neither of us are aware of."

She threw him a disbelieving look. "I do believe you're being too kind, my lord. But I agree, we should wait to find out exactly what is the situation regarding this estate and then move forward from there."

He nodded, but the dejected slump of her shoulders left him uneasy. "If the home does fall into my hands, my lady, I'm more than willing to gift the estate to you if it means so very much to you." What was he saying? He needed the funds that the estate would bring in to secure the future of his son and his own Scottish estates. Lady Zetland and her wretched visage had made him soft in the head.

"Oh, no, my lord. I could never accept such a gift, but thank you for offering. That was very kind of you."

He wasn't kind—he felt like a brute kicking a lone woman out of her home. No money was worth doing such an underhanded thing and he would not in this case. Not if she did not have anywhere to go.

"I will send for my lawyer straight away to see what has happened. And I suppose," she said, rolling up the document once again, "since this is your home, I should offer for you to stay while we sort out this problem and decide on what I shall do. There are plenty of rooms, it would be no trouble. We're family, after all."

In a way they were family, but still, Marcus didn't like the fact that Lady Zetland made him feel like a green lad before a beautiful woman for the first time. "If it's no trouble. As I said, I'll be leaving in a week or so, once this debacle is dealt with to everyone's satisfaction. I never meant to boot you out on your ass, my lady."

Her eyes widened, and Marcus recalled that his Scottish way of speaking probably wasn't something her ladyship had ever heard before.

A chuckle floated toward him and he glanced up to see her laughing. Perhaps she wasn't such a proper English miss.

"Apologies, my lady. I've lived on my own for many years, and I'm not used to being around titled gentlefolk."

She smiled, and the breath in his lungs seized. Holy God, she was too beautiful for words. Although he could think of some: angelic, pure, a rose in full bloom…

"Do not trouble yourself, Lord Zetland, do not change yourself on my account. I can assure you that I've heard worse."

"You have?" He highly doubted it. "Where, may I ask?"

"My mother for many years has been part of the London Relief Society, a place that helps children learn and move on into employment, both in London and in the country. The last few years before I married, my mama included me in the meetings, took me out to the schools and shelters which by then also helped women move on from less savoury means of earning a living to a more respectable, safe one. So I have heard worse than ass, I can assure you."

"Your mother sounds like a woman of great kindness."

"She is," her ladyship said, smiling wistfully. "And I'm afraid that once she hears of my losing Kewell Hall, she'll be on the doorstep within a few days demanding to know what it's all about."

"I should be scared then?" Marcus asked, only half seriously.

"Oh yes, you should be terrified. The Duchess of Athelby is not someone even I would like to go up against."

Marcus swallowed. Lady Zetland was the Duke of

Athelby's daughter. Good God, he'd heard of the Duke and Duchess of Athelby all the way up in Scotland. They practically ran the haute ton. He'd heard his distant cousin had married well, but he hadn't known just how well.

"I consider myself duly warned, my lady," he said, standing. "Do you mind if I retire to my room? I've travelled many miles today and I must admit I'd like to freshen up before dinner."

"Of course," Lady Zetland said, standing and walking over to the fire and ringing the staff bell. Within a moment the footman who'd opened the front door was back, standing to attention and ready to do whatever the mistress of the house decreed.

Marcus had to chuckle at the ways of the English, especially compared to how he lived. He was a simple man. He may live in a castle, but half of it was falling down about his ears, although in time the rents from the English properties would help in restoration of his home. He was titled in his own right in Scotland—the laird of Clan Duncan—but to be laird was nothing like it once was in the Highlands, and the clan today was nothing like it once was either.

"I dine at eight sharp." She walked him to the library door and pointed to a room across the hall. "The dining room is through there, Lord Zetland."

"Please," he said, turning to her. "Call me Marcus. We're family, distant as that may be."

She smiled and again he had to tear his gaze away from her beauty. When he returned to Scotland he would have to find himself a bride, or a tumble. This visceral reaction he had to Lady Zetland was not common, certainly not for him, and it could only mean one thing. He needed a woman.

"I would like that, Marcus. Thank you. In turn, you may call me Henrietta."

He nodded then followed the footman out of the room and upstairs. He liked the name Henrietta, or Hetti as it was shortened to in Scotland. It made him wonder if that was what her close friends called her, or what her husband used to. It suited her, and with time maybe they too would become friends and she would allow him to call her by such a name as well.

CHAPTER 3

Later that evening, Henrietta paced before the fireplace, the pearls about her neck a lovely distraction running through her hands as she thought about tonight's dinner. The idea of having dinner with her husband's cousin wouldn't normally rattle her so, but the man who'd walked into her library—all six foot six of him she was sure, with shoulders that looked strong enough to haul two women upon them to his chamber for who knows what—was not someone she'd thought to be dining with.

Her body had not been her own upon meeting him, and reluctantly she had to admit to feeling a tidbit of attraction to him that was both confusing and complicating in equal parts.

She recalled the dinners she'd had with her husband Walter, and the times he'd mentioned who would inherit if they did not produce a child, which unfortunately in the short year that they were married they had not. Not that Henrietta had any hope of producing an heir. Her one regret about marrying the marquess was having lied to him.

Walter had talked of Marcus Duncan as nothing more than a distant cousin who would never impact on their life. After today his impact was well felt, and Henrietta's heart still hadn't calmed after meeting him. She suppressed the unexpected nerves that fluttered in her stomach and steeled herself for the forthcoming meal.

The dinner gong sounded below stairs and her maid Mary handed her a shawl. Henrietta thanked her and headed downstairs, concentrating on her breathing and ignoring the havoc in her stomach. She'd been out of society for some time, so it was only natural that the first gentleman to call upon her would make her react in such a nonsensical way. His stay was for only a week. He'd be gone soon enough and then her life would be back to normal.

This afternoon she'd sent an express to her solicitor in London to find out if the paperwork Lord Zetland had showed her today was correct, and if so, how they had been so lax in their handling of her affairs.

Had she known this home was no longer hers she would've moved to the estate she owned not far from here —a lovely country manor house that her parents had gifted her upon her eighteenth birthday, a place she could always go to should the need arise.

It had certainly arisen now.

As much as she would miss her home here at Kewell Hall, a residence where she and Walter had created many happy memories, her own home in Surrey also held fond memories. It was after all where she'd met Walter for the first time, when her parents held a ball there during her first season. It was where Walter had proposed. So if she did lose this house, all would be well in the end.

She clasped the railing of the stairs and, picking up her gown, started making her way downstairs. Halfway down the library door opened and Lord Zetland entered the hall before her. Dressed in a Scottish kilt of deep red and blue, the towering Highlander looked like he'd stepped out of the pages of history. His shirt was tucked into his kilt, the sporran about his hips accentuated his narrow waist, and he wore a dinner jacket over his shirt. Never had she seen a Scotsman look so handsome.

Lord Zetland was all man. There were no soft edges or dandy traits about this gentleman—he was hard, strong, capable. His jaw was angular and looked chiselled to perfection, a god in a kilt, and his hair had the slightest hint of gold through his darker locks, but his eyes were his best feature. They were kind, thoughtful, knowledgeable she would bet, and she doubted he ever missed much that went on before him.

"Good evening, Marcus. You look wonderful. Is that your family kilt you're wearing?"

"Aye, Henrietta, 'tis so." He held out his hand to her. His clasp was warm, gentler than she thought it would be, before he placed her hand onto his arm and escorted her in to dine.

"I asked cook to do up a few Scottish dishes, so I hope you like haggis."

He chuckled, holding out her chair before seating himself across from her. Even the expanse of polished cedar that separated them wasn't nearly far enough to stop the blood in her veins from reacting to his nearness.

Maybe her mama was correct and she needed to return to town, throw herself back into the social whirl of the ton, and continue her mourning away from isolation. She'd been here for just over a year, most of that time alone, other than when her parents or brother visited. Her reaction to the Highlander was proof that she needed to leave, if only for a few months.

The first course, a soup called a la Solferino, was placed before them and for a time they ate in silence, before Henrietta looked up and caught Marcus studying her.

She dabbed her mouth with her napkin. "Is something the matter with the soup, my lord?"

"No," he said, grinning at her mischievously. "I was only thinking that I'd not dined with a woman for quite some time, and how much I missed doing so. My home is quite isolated and I do not travel away from there much, so to be dining with you—a duke's daughter, a marchioness in your own right—well, 'tis a novelty I'll not soon forget."

How sweet he was. His heartfelt words made her lips twitch. "You're not alone in your thoughts of how nice it is to dine with someone. I was thinking the same myself, and that perhaps no matter whether I keep this home or retire to my own estate, it's probably time I returned to London to see my family and regain the life I lost when Walter passed away."

"You have your own estate. May I enquire as to where?"

Henrietta notified the servants to take away their first course and bring in the second. "I do, three miles from Kewell Hall in fact. If I do lose this estate I shall make Cranfield my home and travel to and from London from there. It is only a short horse ride from here if you would like to visit it during your stay. I don't mind, truly. I've been meaning to check on it for some days, and I could show you a little of this estate too on our ride. Kill two birds with one stone."

"A good hard ride is just what I need."

Henrietta hid her grin behind her napkin at his words, and as the second course was placed before them, she glimpsed the reddening of Lord Zetland's cheeks. "Are you well, my lord? You look a little flushed."

He cleared his throat. "I'm very well, thank you. The fire behind me is a little warm, 'tis all."

"Is tomorrow too soon for you? Kewell Hall's estate is very beautiful, and should you end up being owner of the property at least you'll know a little of its layout."

"I would like that very much," he said, a half smile tweaking his lips.

Henrietta caught herself a little obsessed with his mouth, his full, soft-looking mouth. Did Marcus kiss with passion or sweet seduction? Passion, she would guess. Any woman in his arms would be devoured, seduced, and made love to wildly. As wild as the Highlands that he hailed from.

The thought shamed her and she turned back to her meal. After Walter's death, she'd not thought to marry again, to allow the opposite sex to impact on her life. It had only been twelve months. Was it too soon for her to be reacting to another man in this way? That she couldn't answer, but deep down she knew Walter would want her to be happy. Not to lock herself away in Surrey and only live half a life.

She glanced down at her wedding band that she still wore. "It's settled then," she said, forking a piece of duck. "I will have the stable staff notified and we'll head off after we break our fast in the morning."

Lord Zetland nodded and the remainder of the meal was pleasant if not a little quiet at times. Not that those pauses of chatter were awkward—on the contrary, they were anything but, and gave Henrietta time to study the new marquess some more.

Who was he? Did he have a young woman in Scotland that he wanted to marry? Had he already been married? He'd certainly not mentioned a wife, so she didn't think that was the case. But he didn't seem to say much about his home, other than it being a castle. He was a mystery, a Scottish one, but one that she would venture to learn more about during his stay here—if only to fulfil her own curiosity, that wanted to know everything, and now.

CHAPTER 4

The grounds and surrounding property of Kewell Hall were magnificent, and the more Marcus saw of the estate, the more he liked what he saw—including the woman who rode alongside him showing him what could possibly be his.

For a woman who looked to have lost the estate, she was being a good sport about it all. Maybe it was simply because she had an estate not far from here and was a duke's daughter, and so Kewell Hall wasn't of such great importance to her. Although, taking in the grounds and the property, he could see she was one widow who took great care to ensure both the home and lands were well tended.

They stopped before a running stream. A little way along, Marcus could see where carriages made the crossing, and the road leading toward the estate.

"This is where Kewell Hall's lands end, and my estate begins. This stream isn't deep, but if it storms it does become so, so always be careful."

He smiled, liking the fact that she needed to warn him

against such things. It was nice to be fussed over, even if only in a little way such as a warning about floods. He'd not been fussed over for a few years, and the emotion it evoked within him, warm and comforting, was a feeling he could get used to.

"Duly noted, my lady."

"Henrietta, please." She threw him a marked gaze and pushed her horse on to cross the stream.

Marcus followed and kicked his mount a little to get him to trot up the slight incline on the other side. They rode to the top of a hill, and the view that opened out onto the valley beyond was magnificent. Acres and acres of trees and grassland where sheep and deer roamed. Marcus took in the vista, admitting to himself that it was pretty good, even if it was England. And then he saw her home. Nestled within a copse of trees sat Cranfield.

If he had been expecting a small estate, he was sorely mistaken. This home was bigger than Kewell Hall. Hundreds of windows glistened in the morning sunlight, and from here he could see two gardeners working in the grounds.

"Your estate is magnificent, Henrietta," he said, settling his mount as it dug at the soil, impatient to continue. "Seeing it, I'm surprised that you don't live there. It is much bigger than Kewell Hall."

She looked back at her estate and shrugged. "It's too large, and although Walter did give me the choice whether to live here or at his estate, I wanted our life to be at Kewell Hall."

"You wanted your children to be raised under the same roof as their father was. There is nothing wrong with your choice."

At the mention of children her gaze shuttered and all of a sudden she seemed sad. Of course he knew they had no children, or he wouldn't be exactly where he was now, a marquess, but maybe they'd just not had enough time to produce an heir. Walter had after all died very young and only a year into their marriage.

"One day perhaps it'll be filled with the sound of children's laughter," he added.

"Perhaps. Now," she said, once again smiling and at ease with him. "Shall we continue? I always give my horse a run from here. Do you wish to do the same?"

Marcus was never one to turn down a challenge. "Aye, of course."

Before he had a chance to prepare himself, Henrietta had spurred her horse into a canter that soon turned into a full-fledged gallop down the hill. He watched her, forgetting for a moment that they were supposed to be racing. Then he started after her, and his horse, a well-bred gelding that had won a few Scottish derbies, was soon only a few paces behind her.

Her laughter floated to him, and he looked ahead only to see her checking his whereabouts.

"You'll have to do better than that, Lord Zetland, to catch me."

He smiled, enjoying himself way too much considering he was supposed to be concentrating on the lands, not racing about the fields with an English marchioness. Even with the lack of highlands to make the view more pleasing, the sight of Henrietta's perfect derriere in her riding attire did compensate well enough for his liking.

They slowed as they crossed a shallow stream and then, following Henrietta's lead, he pulled his mount into a slow trot then a walk. "Your horse is fast, I will give you that, but had you not cheated and taken off before I was ready, I would've had you beat."

She grinned, patting her horse's neck. "I need no head start to win, do not fool yourself, my lord."

He chuckled. "I shall not argue with you, my lady. I see you're not ready yet to listen to common sense on the matter." He grinned at her affront and laughed when she understood his mirth. To be happy, carefree as she was right at this moment, suited her very well, and never had he seen a prettier woman.

They came clear of a copse of trees and her home rose before them. Built in a similar style to Kewell Hall, the Georgian property's sandstone all but glowed in the morning sun, inviting and homely. And yet no footman came to greet them, no servants. Only the yard staff walked about, going about their duties.

Marcus dismounted and came about to help Henrietta, but found her already beside her horse. She caught his gaze, shrugging. "Thank you for thinking of me, but I've been dismounting on my own for some time now. I'll even surprise you in a little while and climb back on without assistance as well."

He bowed. "You'll have my full attention so I may see that."

They tied the horses to a nearby tree, and started toward the front door. "There isn't any staff within the house itself. They're employed at Kewell Hall now, but the housekeeper does send over maids to keep the dust at bay." She pulled a key out of a pocket in her riding habit and unlocked the door, swinging it wide.

"And this is Cranfield." She turned toward him. "What do you think?"

Marcus entered and looked about. The home was similar to Kewell Hall, except this home was cloaked in dust sheets, the window shutters closed, the sound of life, of people living within the walls, not echoing around them.

Outside the house looked welcoming, inside it looked desolate.

"It is lovely, lass. If not a little lonely, I would think. Why did you not let this property out once you were settled at Kewell Hall?"

Henrietta strode through the foyer and started toward the back of the home. He followed. "I don't know. I suppose I wanted to keep it for myself. It was given to me, after all, and I have so many memories here. I'd hate to lease the property out, allow another family to form their own wonderful memories, only for me to turn around in a few years and tell them they must leave. To do such a thing would upset me, and so instead I closed it up, left her waiting for me when I was ready to return."

The home seemed to suit her, and as little as Marcus knew the Marchioness of Zetland, even he could see she was relaxed and at ease here.

"This is my favourite room, and it was where my grandmother spent most of her time. It's also rumoured that she was proposed to here by King George IV, but she would never confirm or deny the story so it's something we'll never know." She grinned at him and something thumped hard in Marcus's chest. He could well understand his cousin's attraction to the woman—she was certainly likeable in all ways, in temperament, character, and appearance.

"My home in Scotland has many clan stories, dating back to Robert the Bruce, but the Scottish ruler never proposed to anyone in my family. As much as some of my ancestors would've loved to have such a tale to tell around a roaring hearth late at night. My son certainly loves swords and all things medieval."

She sat on a settee that was covered in dust cloths and gestured for him to join her. He did, chucking a little when a poof of dust permeated the air as they made themselves comfortable.

"You have a son? I did not know you were married. Is your wife still in Scotland?"

"Arthur is his name, a fine strapping lad of two years of age. His mother is no longer with us," he said, shying away from the brutal truth that the boy's mother had left without a by-your-leave. Or the fact that he'd not had the chance to marry the lass and bring some respectability to his son's birth.

"I'm very sorry for your loss," she said, touching his hand quickly. "Tell me then, what is your Scottish home like?" she asked, changing the subject, which he was glad of. "My mother has a property there which I love visiting. I haven't been for two or so years, but intend to make the journey before next season."

"My home, Morleigh Castle, sits upon the mountain range overlooking Loch Ruthven. I can see the loch from two sides of the castle and in winter, the peaks are covered in snow. The area is marshy, so 'tis hard to travel at certain times of the year. The castle itself is cold, full of passageways and ghouls, or so my servants say. You're more than welcome to stay should you travel up that far within the country. I'd love the company." And he would love *her* company above anything else. A light blush stole across her cheeks and for the life of him he could not look away.

She sighed, leaning back and laying her head against the settee's back, staring at the ceiling. "I think I shall take you up on that offer, Lord Zetland. The thought of traveling to London and taking part in another season does little to tempt me. I miss my friends, but they can survive some more months without my company. I should so like to travel a little more before the endless nights and days of socializing take up my time and a holiday to the Highlands becomes nothing but a dream."

The thought of Henrietta returning to town, or being courted by eligible gentlemen, left him somewhat annoyed. He didn't want to think about it, and that in itself was worth pondering. Even his son's mother had not brought forth in Marcus this uneasy feeling that should he pursue this woman, she could turn out to be part of his future. Part of his lad's future. He'd always wanted a wife, and Henrietta with her calm and generous nature would make a wonderful mother to his child and any that they would have together.

Marcus looked out toward the back gardens from where they sat and shook the thought aside. He'd only known the woman two days and already he was planning to make her into his brood mare. Did he have rocks in his head? She may not ever wish to marry again, let alone marry him.

Marriage! He really needed to get a grasp on his wayward imaginings.

"Morleigh Castle will always welcome ye, Lady Zetland. You need not even announce your impending arrival."

She turned and met his gaze. "You're being too kind." She studied him a moment. "I have to ask, Lord Zetland. You're an eligible gentleman now—is there not someone pining for you at home?"

"Dinna worry about that, I have no lass waiting for me."

Henrietta frowned. "I find that hard to believe."

He chuckled. How wrong she was. "Do ye think me handsome enough then to tempt the ladies? I shall take that as a compliment."

"You're putting words into my mouth, my lord, as well you know."

He was indeed, and yet he liked sparring with her. She was a worthy opponent.

"Your son, is he well behaved? I should imagine being away from him all these weeks is difficult?"

"He's very well and much loved. I miss him more than I thought I would, and it was one of the reasons why I didna travel from Scotland after Lord Zetland's death. The lad was only a year old then, and I didna feel it was right for me to leave him alone to travel so very far away. But I only have a week left here, so not too much longer before I see him again."

"Does he look like you?" she asked. "I bet he's handsome."

Marcus raised his brow, unable to let such a question pass him by. "There ye go again, hinting at my good looks," he teased. He looked at her and their gazes locked. Held. And a tension that simmered between them, had done so since the moment they met, thrummed hard, and it took all of Marcus's control not to lean across the small space that separated them and take her lips.

Damn, he wanted to kiss her.

"I'm not a green miss, my lord. I can admit when a gentleman is handsome or no, and you sir are as handsome as any I've seen. Terribly shocking for a marchioness and a duke's daughter to say, but my upbringing was not conventional and my parents always taught us to speak our minds and stand up for what we believe in."

"I like those traits. They do you justice."

"I hope so," she said, slapping her hands on her knees and standing. "Now, we'd best return to Kewell Hall before luncheon. I have a surprise for you today."

Did the sweetness of the woman never end? She was a

marvel and he couldn't help but be charmed by her proper English manners. "You do not have to go to any lengths to please me. I'm content just to visit, get to know you and those who live and work at Kewell Hall. You need not go out of your way for me."

"Oh, I haven't, I've simply had a special meal prepared for you for lunch. I think you'll enjoy it."

Please don't be haggis again. As Scottish as he was, the thought of boiled lungs, heart and liver stuffed into a sheep's gut was more than enough to make his stomach roil. It had been bad enough having to eat it the previous evening. "Can you tell me what it is?" If it was haggis, he would have to mentally prepare himself for the torture that was about to unfold.

"No, you'll see soon enough. Now come, I want to show you an old monastery nearby that is fascinating and also supposedly haunted. Since your castle seems to be also, maybe you could give me your professional opinion on this."

He chuckled. "Lead the way, my lady. If there are sprits or ghouls to be found, I'll know it."

The remainder of the day was a day worth living— good company, great conversation, a picnic luncheon of cold meats and wine down beside the river, and an outing that was worth Marcus's time. He could not remember the last time he'd enjoyed himself so much with a woman, and a woman that he wasn't courting. Not that Henrietta wasn't a bonny lass, for she certainly was that, but with her being a new widow, twelve months may be too soon for her to really move on from the loss of her husband. And Marcus wasn't really sure he wanted a wife at this stage in his life.

He was still young, only eight and twenty. As much as he'd like to have more children someday, he also didn't want to rush into anything simply because Lady Zetland encompassed all that he'd ever wanted in a partner.

No, he would return to Scotland, and if their paths happened to cross again, then he'd know fate had stepped in and pushed their hand. Otherwise, mayhap they were not meant to be.

CHAPTER 5

Henrietta lay on her bed late that night and all that she saw before her was Lord Zetland—Marcus, as he'd asked her to call him—and his delectable backside as he'd climbed up the old monastery ruins, reaching back down to help her join him on the little lookout created by a crumbling wall.

She smiled recalling the enjoyment of the day, the carefree conversation that was not stilted or hard fought. They seemed to talk quite naturally together, found similar things amusing, and his love for the land, even if Kewell Hall turned out to be hers after all, was genuine. He showed that he cared for her discussions about planting, harvest, and the tenant farmers. Wanted to know her plans, what the yield was like and the local community.

Even the thought of losing this home and property wasn't so upsetting if she knew it would go to a man who would care for it as much as she had. The fact that they would be neighbors as well was not disturbing either. In fact, she could ride over to Kewell Hall very easily, to visit, help his lordship out if he needed, and see the servants again, make sure they were happy.

She rolled over, shaking her head at her own musings. Who was she kidding? The only reason she'd come over to Kewell Hall would be to see Marcus, and the possibility of seeing him in his breeches, perhaps bending over before a fire while he stoked it.

She really shouldn't be thinking about him in such a way—he was her husband's distant cousin, and heir. Although Walter had been gone over a year, was she being callous, disrespecting her marriage vows, to be thinking about another man in such a way? Not that she would marry him. He'd not shown one morsel of attraction to her, except perhaps that one look they shared in her library at Cranfield, but otherwise he'd been the perfect gentleman.

He was a young man, and although they were similar in age, he would no doubt wish for more children one day, and that she could never give him. It was her one shame that she carried with her and had not even been able to tell Walter of, even after their marriage.

To be barren, unable to conceive—as her London doctor had told her—had been a devastating blow, but not one that she did not see coming. She had known since she started to grow into a woman that something was not quite right, and had asked her mother for advice. That she would never bear children was not what they'd expected to hear. Still, she'd had her season, caught the eye of a marquess and married him, all the while hoping the doctors had been wrong. But after a year of marriage, she'd not once had her menses, and so it would seem nor would she have a child.

She pushed back her blankets and slipped out of bed, wrapped a shawl about her shoulders and left her room.

The house was dark, besides the few candles left burning that would soon flicker out due to their own wax burning down to nothing.

Picking up a small candlestick, she started down the stairs and made for the kitchen, intending to pour herself a glass of milk and maybe see if her cook had any freshly baked bread she could snack on.

Entering the kitchen she stifled a scream as she saw the shadowed figure of Lord Zetland sitting at the table, a cup with some sort of beverage clasped tight in his hands. He stood quickly, the scrape of the chair on the slate floor loud in the room, and she cringed, not wanting to wake the staff and have them find them alone.

"You could not sleep either, lass?" he asked, gesturing to a chair for her to sit and join him. Henrietta checked the pantry first for bread, and smiled when she spotted a freshly baked loaf. Cutting a slice, she placed it on a plate and set it on the table before pouring herself a cup of milk and joining his lordship in his midnight snack.

"I could not. I do not know why, since we had such a busy day, but for whatever reason sleep eludes me."

She shot his lordship a quick glance and thanked the shadowed room they were in. Her cheeks burned with what she saw. Lord Zetland wore nothing but a shirt and breeches, but the shirt was open at the neck, so much so that she could see the outline of his chest and the light frosting of dark hair.

She'd not seen a man in such a state of dress for over a year. But looking at this Lord Zetland was so different than looking at her own dearly departed husband's body. Although the late Lord Zetland had been tall, he was also of a wiry figure. He'd had muscles of course, but the current Lord Zetland, who was slowly sipping his coffee, his muscles...well, they were quite profound and filled out his shirt with ease.

Henrietta slipped another bite of bread into her mouth and chewed, anything to keep her eyes from darting back to his marvellous figure that she could see quite well now that her eyes had adjusted to the room.

"You can look at me, Henrietta. I will not bite." He grinned at her and her cheeks heated further.

"I am looking at you," she said, wishing she could pull the words back as soon as she said them. "That is to say, what an odd thing to say, for I have been looking at you. Why do you think I've not been?" But she already knew why he'd asked, because she'd been peeping at him like a delicious naughty novelty before her, as if looking at him was forbidden to her even though she kept sneaking glances.

"You usually can meet my gaze, and yet right now you can barely lift your eyes past my chest."

Henrietta did meet his gaze then, and she didn't miss the simmering heat that lurked in his blue orbs. She'd thought he'd been making light of their situation, of them being in a darkened kitchen, half dressed and alone. But he wasn't. Instead, he was looking at her in a way that she'd not even seen Walter look at her in the depths of night when they were alone. His gaze dropped to her lips and then further over her person, and a shiver stole over her body, making her breasts feel heavy and tight beneath her shift. Her heart was beating too fast to be proper.

"And yet I find right at this moment that your eyes too are not meeting mine, my lord. Do you like what you see?" What was she saying? What on earth was she doing? Never had she been so forward, or scandalous. A little voice whispered that her mother would be so proud of her right at this moment. The duchess was a woman who lived life to the fullest, wanted her children to also, but Henrietta had always been proper, comported herself as the correct daughter of a duke. But in the company of Lord Zetland, something niggled within her to be naughty, to play and laugh for once instead of the opposite.

His gaze darkened further and he placed down his cup. "Very much so." His voice was deep, just above a whisper, and she shivered and then started when he pushed back his chair. "Good night, Lady Zetland."

She watched him go, shutting her mouth with a snap as he closed the kitchen door behind him. Well, she wasn't quite sure what had just happened, and she wasn't entirely sure that she liked Lord Zetland leaving without continuing the enlightening conversation they were just partaking in. Not to mention that the thought of him liking what he saw left her nerves frazzled.

The idea that she would have to speak to him upon the morrow would be awkward and not something to look forward to now. After what they'd said to each other, if he thought her meeting his gaze right now had been a problem, he had not seen anything yet.

MARCUS RODE HARD toward the river that ran about Kewell Hall. The day he and Henrietta had ridden out to her estate, she'd told him that Kewell Hall sat surrounded by a waterway that forked off and ran about the estate, making it almost surrounded by a moat.

The sky bore ominous clouds, and in the distance he could hear the rumbling of thunder, even with the thumping of hooves beneath him. He crossed the stream and had just started up the other side of the embankment when the heavens opened, the heavy, cold rain making his vision less than he'd like. He pulled his horse up, planning to return home to be safe.

Out of the corner of his eye a flash of blue caught his eye and he looked over to see Henrietta pulled up under an old oak, trying to find what little cover she could during the storm.

Lady Zetland looked a treat atop her horse, her figure to full advantage, her seat straight, her chin held high with authority, no doubt from being brought up under a ducal roof.

He started over toward her. He'd not looked forward to seeing her today, not after his atrocious behaviour the night before. What had come over him to have asked her what she thought of him he'd never know. That she'd not looked at him with any yearning since he'd been under her roof had been driving him to distraction, and the more time he spent with her, the more he wanted her to see him. To want him as much as he was fearing that he wanted her.

Henrietta being the daughter of a duke meant that before he even thought of courting a woman of such rank, he had better be sure that she was the woman for him and open to such pursuits—two points that he was not certain of. Which made his taunting words the night before wicked and completely unacceptable.

He pulled up his mount beside her and threw her a half smile. "Lady Zetland, I must apologize for last night. I should never have teased you so, questioned you about where your gaze was situated. It was very wrong of me, and I'm sorry, lass."

She smiled at him and it went some way to dispel his shame. "Do not be embarrassed, Lord Zetland. Your question when all told was on point. I was looking at you, scandalously so, thinking of what lay beneath your shirt and what it would be like to kiss you. So you see," she said, looking back at the weather that continued to gather in strength and ferocity, "I'm not embarrassed or angry at your words and I do not want our open and honest conversations to end because of them."

Marcus stared at her a moment, the breath in his lungs awfully shallow. Did that mean… "You imagined kissing me, Lady Zetland?"

She nodded, biting her lip a little. A small droplet of rain dripped off her chin and her words broke what little restraint he had. Moving his horse to come up beside her, he reached across the space, clasped her cheeks, and kissed her. Hard.

Her cool lips met his, and instead of a woman of rank who did not know how to kiss, he was met by a woman who clasped the lapels of his coat, held him close, and kissed him back with such passion, such need, that it made his head spin.

He shouldn't be doing this. A warning went off in his mind. Henrietta was his deceased cousin's wife. A duke's daughter, a woman who may not want him when she learned of his shame. That his son was illegitimate and birthed from a woman who was in his employ. If she could not accept his son, then he could not make her his. It was one absolute truth that could not be broken in his life.

The kiss went on, their tongues meshed, teased. The kiss slowed and sped up, provoked and beseeched them both for more wonderful things that could be had in bed if they ended up there.

His mount shifted under him and broke them apart. The distance made him relinquish his hold but for the life of him he could not stop looking at her. Her cheeks were flushed, her lips a little swollen from their embrace, and the need in her eyes pulled at a part of him he'd not thought existed. He rubbed his chest, trying to calm his racing heart.

"I suppose now I need to apologize for that kiss, and yet, as much as I should say I'm sorry for taking you in my arms and kissing you, I'm not sorry at all. I've wanted to kiss you since the moment I arrived."

Her lips twitched and again her gaze dipped to his chest, just as it had the night before. "I've wanted to kiss you as well."

A crack of thunder sounded and the rain started down heavier than before.

Henrietta kicked her mount a little to leave the shelter of the oak. Marcus followed. "We'd better cross the river again before it's flooded and we have no way of returning to the estate."

"Of course." They rode as fast as the sodden ground would allow, and only slowed as they came to the river. Although it was a little faster in its flow, it was still passable at this time from the looks of it.

"Follow me here, Lord Zetland, and the horse will keep its footing."

He did as she bade, starting to wonder whether he would comply with whatever she asked of him. The Lady Zetland was a woman worth following anywhere.

CHAPTER 6

Henrietta sat at her desk and scribbled a note to her mother, leaving out the tidbit of information that she'd kissed a man who was not her husband, boldly, wantonly, and with little regard to what anyone thought.

When he'd instigated the kiss she'd thought for a instant to pull away, but the moment his lips touched hers, all thoughts of denying him faded away. Now all that she'd thought of since was doing it again, of when she'd see him privately, and where this newfound intimacy may lead. The idea of him sharing her bed, his strong, capable hands running over her body. Why even now, when he was out with the estate's steward looking over the tenant farms, her stomach fluttered at the thought of bedding him.

To think of what they could do if she allowed such liberties made the breath in her lungs seize. To picture him above her, bare of clothes, his strong muscles flexing with the effort to bring her pleasure… She shut her eyes, liking the imagining more than any well-bred young woman should.

A knock at the door startled her and she jumped in her

chair, the sound of a footman requesting admission bringing her thoughts back to her duties. Henrietta folded her missive and pulling out the top drawer, placed the letter to her mama inside.

"Come in," she said, shutting the drawer and locking it.

"The new housemaid has arrived, Lady Zetland. Did you wish to meet with her now, or at another time?"

"Send her in, thank you." Henrietta stood as the young woman entered, her bright red hair hardly tamed by her hasty tying back. The maid bobbed a quick curtsy, but didn't venture to smile.

"Lady Zetland, thank ye for your employment. I will not disappoint ye."

Henrietta smiled, coming around her desk to lessen the space between them. "Have your duties been explained to you, and what I expect from all the staff here at Kewell Hall?"

The young woman nodded. "The housekeeper has told me of my duties and where I shall sleep."

She was a pretty woman, and Scottish. It would seem that this week she was to be surrounded by those that hailed from the northern region.

"Your name?" she asked.

The woman met her gaze. "Miss Emma Campbell, my lady."

"And what part of Scotland are you from, Miss Campbell?"

The young woman looked about the room a little before answering. "The Highlands, my lady."

Henrietta smiled. "A lovely part of the country if ever there was one." She walked the new maid toward the library door. "Mrs. King will take you from here. I wish you well with your employment here."

The woman dipped into a neat curtsy. "Thank you, my lady. I feel it shall be."

Henrietta watched Mrs. King take her toward the kitchens where no doubt she'd be put to work once the staff had partaken in their luncheon.

The front door opened and in strolled Lord Zetland from his outing with the steward. His hair was mussed from riding all morning, and a shiver of delight stole over her at seeing him again. After their kiss, one that had encompassed more passion than she'd ever experienced before, all her thoughts were consolidated to when they would do it again.

By the looks of his gaze, dark and full of promise, their time to kiss would happen sooner rather than later.

"Lord Zetland. Did you find the tenant farms well tended?"

He handed his grey redingote to a waiting footman, along with his hat and gloves.

"I did, Lady Zetland. They all seem to be in good hands and well tended, just as you said they were." He strode past her, but surprisingly, he clasped her hand and pulled her into the library.

He shut the door behind them, and the moment the door slammed closed he pushed her up against the door, her face clasped between his capable hands as his mouth, hot and insistent, took her lips, pulling forth in her a hunger she'd not known she had.

No sooner had their kiss started than it ended, and for a moment Henrietta held the door handle to steady her feet.

He ran a finger down her cheek, tipping up her chin to meet his gaze. "All day, the entire time that I rode about the estate, all my thoughts were on you. Of seeing you again, of kissing you. I find that from the moment I wake, to the moment I fall asleep, my mind is occupied with nothing but your sweetness."

Henrietta bit her lip, delighted at his sweet words. Had she the ability to speak, she would've told Marcus that she'd done little other than think of him as well. Counting down the hours until he returned to the estate so they might pick up where they'd ended their tryst the day before.

"Your kisses are wicked, my lord, and worse than that, you know how much they affect me."

"They affect ye, do they lass? How so?" he asked, dipping his head and kissing his way along her cheek, her ear, paying attention to her lobe for a moment before kissing down her neck. Oh dear lord. She swallowed as her body yearned with hunger for him to do more. How was she ever to concentrate on his question and answer it when his lips teased her so?

She pushed at his chest a little so she could see him and not be so unfocused. "I loved my husband, I truly did, but although the marriage bed was enjoyable—or at least I thought it was—it wasn't long into our marriage that Walter became ill. So you see, Lord Zetland, I'm at a disadvantage compared to you. I'm not as worldly about such things."

He grinned and she went back into his arms, needing to be close to him again. "I'll not rush you, lass. We're only kissing after all."

Henrietta nodded, wanting more than to kiss the man. A scandalous way of thinking, but in his arms she couldn't think of any place she'd rather be. There was little chance of her falling pregnant should they end up lovers and so nothing ruinous could occur if she did take him to her bed.

A pang of sadness swamped her that falling pregnant wasn't a concern when it really ought to be. Had she grown correctly as the doctor told her, then Lord Zetland would need to be careful. "You're all gentlemanly behavior, my lord," she said, running her hand through the hair at his nape.

"I'm no gentleman. Far from it, lass."

She bit her lip, the deep tone of his words making her ache in places she'd not known could ache. How enlightening. "How so? Show me," she said, stepping closer still so her breasts touched his chest.

MARCUS SWALLOWED AND, about to claim his prize, inwardly swore when there was a light knock on the door with the accompanying sound of female voices. Whoever it was who'd arrived made Henrietta's eyes widen in shock and panic and she shushed him, gesturing for him to sit on the settee near the fire.

He did as she asked, as quietly as he could, while she fought to right her gown and hair which had become a little mussed after their kiss. He couldn't help but watch and grin at her hasty attempt to make herself proper, when all he wanted to do was make her anything but.

She opened the door, delight crossing her features at the sight of whoever stood there. "Mama, how lovely to see you. I didn't know that you were going to visit me. I was just composing a letter to you."

Marcus stood, clasping his hands behind his back as the Duchess of Athelby and another woman walked into the room. The duchess took in the room, and her gaze, sharp and knowledgeable, fixed on him. He fought not to shuffle on his feet at her cool stare, and was relieved when Henrietta walked toward him after greeting the other woman.

"Mama, Margaret, may I introduce Lord Zetland, the

new marquess. Lord Zetland, this is my mama, the Duchess of Athelby and my cousin, Miss Margaret Bell."

He bowed. "A pleasure to meet you, Your Grace." And he could see where Henrietta gained her beautiful looks, for the duchess was also a handsome woman, even with her age.

"How do you do, Lord Zetland?"

"Very well, thank you, Your Grace," he said, not knowing if her tone was that of friend or foe.

"Lord Zetland is here to see the estate. It seems that I may not be the owner of Kewell Hall after all. Walter didn't sign the paperwork to finalize my inheritance."

Marcus looked to Henrietta as her tone was one of disappointment, and he never wanted that for her. The estate wasn't entailed, and so technically he could gift her the house and lands. But if he did that, the blunt that he could gain by leasing the property to help his son have a more secure future, plus help restore his own Scottish castle, would be gone. But he also didn't want Henrietta to be unhappy. Maybe he should just give it to her and be done with it. He had two other properties to gain income from. He did not need to be selfish.

"About that, my dear," the duchess said, going to sit behind the desk. "You are correct in your assumptions, as Walter did not sign the deed transferring ownership. Our lawyer came to see us, apologizing for the error regarding this matter. You are not the owner of Kewell Hall and its lands or tenant farms. I have come here, with your cousin, to help you shift your things to Cranfield. To open up your home and hire the appropriate staff."

Marcus frowned, not wanting Henrietta to go anywhere, and certainly not three miles away. "There is no rush if what you say is true. Henrietta has been helping me learn how the property and home is run, and to gain trust with the steward and staff. It would be a great impediment if she were to leave now."

The duchess raised one suspicious eyebrow. "Henrietta, is it?" She cleared her throat, throwing her daughter a knowing look. "You have a few days to tie up any loose ends regarding the estate and then my daughter will be moving to Cranfield."

Henrietta sighed, but nodded, and Marcus wanted to swear. He didn't want her to go. The thought gave him pause when something akin to panic took flight in his chest. He'd grown used to seeing her at dinner and breakfast. Their rides about the estate. And now that they were on more private terms, the days of homecomings would be sweeter still. Similar to what had happened this afternoon.

"I shall still be able to help you until you return to Scotland, Lord Zetland. Do not worry."

He nodded, but didn't venture any further words on the matter. The duchess, seemingly pleased with the outcome, stood and walked over to her daughter. "Come, help me to my room and we'll discuss Cranfield."

At the door, Henrietta paused, turning back to Marcus. "See you at dinner, Lord Zetland."

He watched them leave and ran a hand through his hair. There wasn't a lot left for him to learn regarding the estate. Glancing over to the desk, he noted a letter left there. Had the duchess placed it there when she sat? He went over to it and flipped it over. Recognizing his lawyer's scrawl and seal on the back, he broke it open, reading the missive quickly.

It stated what the duchess had just said. Kewell Hall was his in its entirety. His lawyer also stated he would forward the documents proving that was the case to his estate in Scotland. Marcus sat on the chair, having to admit that his time here in England would have to come to an end. Even if the house was leased or he gave it to Henrietta, either way there wasn't anything left to keep him here.

Except the woman that filled his every waking moment and dream state.

Henrietta.

CHAPTER 7

Henrietta sat in the back parlor that overlooked the terrace with her cousin Margaret—Maggie to the family—and told her of her growing infatuation with Lord Zetland. Of her scandalous idea that she wanted to act on regarding the Scottish lord who currently resided under her roof.

"He's certainly handsome, Henrietta, but as someone who's been married to a man who was one way prior to our marriage and then someone entirely different afterwards, I have to ask if you are certain he's not a wolf in sheep's clothing. He's Scottish, and they're not widely known to have a liking for the English, need I remind you," she said, nodding for emphasis.

Henrietta chuckled, but her cousin had good reason for saying such things. She'd been married to the Earl of Worncliffe, a man who turned out to be so violent that Maggie had no other option but to divorce him. Even being related to the Duke of Athelby had not been enough to save her reputation, and Henrietta's mother bringing Maggie here meant only one thing—that she would make Maggie her companion and give the woman some sort of financial security and position, little as that was.

Henrietta didn't like the idea at all. Maggie should be allowed to marry again, go to balls and parties and continue the friendships she had during her marriage. Whilst, Lord Worncliffe walked about London able to do as he pleased and without an ounce of scandal marring his name. Maggie had been stripped of her fortune that she'd brought to the marriage, leaving her with very little to live on. The unfairness of it all was maddening, and Henrietta hated the outcome that had befallen her cousin just for seeking her freedom.

"He's not a bad man. Even if we were to marry—and I can promise you that will not happen—I do not believe he would change. He's kind, very sensual, and his kisses… well, I cannot even think that a man who kisses so well could turn about and be a monster."

Maggie frowned, thinking over Henrietta's words. "This may be true. God knows, Lord Worncliffe could not kiss at all. In fact, it was quite unpleasant."

They both laughed. Then Henrietta said, "If I leave to go to Cranfield it'll mean that I'll not see Marcus as often as I'd like. I do not wish to leave, not yet at least."

"Hmm," Maggie said, frowning. "Maybe I could fake an illness and that will convince your mama to let you stay here a little longer."

"I think you're forgetting that Mama is the Duchess of Athelby. She'll see through our little ruse soon enough. No," Henrietta said, standing to emphasise her words. "I will simply tell her I'm not yet ready to leave and that I shall have her return to town. When Lord Zetland does depart, I'll send for Mama's assistance. You of course, Maggie, may stay."

"Will your mama leave, do you think? I know she'd been looking forward to seeing you again."

As much as Henrietta loved her parents, they did sometimes meddle a little too much in her life. She was a widow, a grown woman, more than capable of looking after herself and deciding when it was time to depart Kewell Hall and Lord Zetland's company. "I will break it to her in a kind way this afternoon. She's resting at present. She will understand, I'm sure of it. Now, I must go and change."

Maggie glanced out the window. "You're not going outside in this heat, are you? You'll freckle."

"There is a garden house down near the river on the western side of the estate, do not forget. Walter's parents had it built not long after they were married. I'll be sure to not stay in the sun for too long, but it's hot enough for a swim today, so I may dip my toes. You're more than welcome to join me if you like."

"No thank you, I shall remain here. I've never been fond of deep, murky water," Maggie said, shivering a little.

Henrietta bid her good afternoon, and after changing into her swimming costume that was conveniently hidden beneath her morning gown she made her way towards the river. The walk only took about fifteen minutes, and with the forest that surrounded the estate, the walk was dappled in sunlight. In the distance she could hear water splashing and her steps slowed as she came out of the trees to the clearing. Here a wooden frame with newly planted climbing roses sat beside the river's edge, a neat and convenient path leading to the water.

But it was who was swimming that caught her full attention. She stopped, biting her lip, as Lord Zetland stood waist-deep in the river, his bare back glowing in the sunlight, water droplets dripping off his hair to run down his perfect form.

"Gosh," she mumbled, not wanting him to spy her and end her delightful inspection of him. The idea that she could swim with him, feel his body next to hers, had her taking the steps needed to reach the garden house. She sat upon the wooden bench beside the door and kicked off her boots.

He turned upon hearing her and smiled as he met her gaze, a wicked light within his eyes. "I had to take the opportunity to swim on this hot day. Are you going to join me, lass?" He ran a hand through his hair, and the muscle in his arm flexed.

She sighed, undoing the buttons at the front of her gown, and Lord Zetland's gaze dropped to her chest. "What are you doing, Henrietta?" he asked after a moment, his voice deeper than she'd ever heard it.

She stood and shuffled out of her gown, leaving the shift and pantalets beneath. Then she pulled off her stockings and laid them over the bench along with her gown. "I'm going for a swim, just like you. This is my swimming costume."

He gaze raked her, his chest rising and falling with each breath. Did the sight of her tempt him, make him want to kiss her again? Oh dear lord she hoped it did, for she'd certainly wanted to kiss him since they were interrupted yesterday when her mother arrived with Maggie.

She took a tentative step into the water and was relieved to find it wasn't too cold. The river had a muddy bed, and she took care walking into the water lest she fall over. "Have you never before seen a woman in a swimming gown, my lord?"

"Och, yes, I've seen women in swimming costumes, my lady. But never a woman who makes me want to rip the swimming costume off their person."

She slipped and landed with a splash in the water, then

came out of the water laughing. "You did that on purpose to distract my concentration."

He swam over to her, pulling her hard against his body and settling her legs about his waist. The action allowed her to feel all the corded muscles in his chest, the heat of his skin, the trickle of water off his chin... "No, I did not, but I also cannot deny the fact that to see you here with me, your swimming costume perfectly transparent now that it's wet, is a boon I'd not thought would happen when I first came down here earlier today."

Henrietta glanced down at her body and her face heated at the sight of her nipples peeking out from her shift. She looked up at the same time Marcus did and realized he too had been looking at her person. Her nipples!

He grinned. "Beautiful."

She slid her hands about his shoulders and kissed him softly. "You have a way with words. I fear I'm not myself with you." She shouldn't allow herself to get involved, to become attached to this man. One could only assume that he'd like to marry again and have more children. And although she could be a loving and generous wife to him, she could not give him children.

"The feeling is mutual, lass." He kissed her and she didn't shy away from the need that thrummed through his body. At her core his hardening manhood pressed insistently against her mons. She could sense the restraint within him as his hands cradled her tight, and all the while his mouth devoured her, kissed her with such passion that she forgot herself and simply gave in to the want for this man. To being a woman in a man's arms, not a duke's daughter in a lord's arms.

He walked them out into deeper water so it lapped at their chests and Henrietta broke the kiss, leaning back to wet her hair. The water was so refreshing, and she'd never had such an experience before with a man. Not even with Walter. Come to think of it, they had not even had a bath together, but the idea of having a bath with Marcus left her achy with need.

She pushed the hair from his face, wanting to see his long eyelashes that made her envious, to see his strong jaw and straight aristocratic nose. There was little doubt in her mind that she wanted Marcus in her bed. To lie with a man that was not her husband. A most scandalous, sinful act, but she could not help it.

She steeled herself to ask for what she wanted without the fear of his denial of her halting her words. Surely after being with him as they now were he would not decline to sleep with her. "If I were to ask you to come to my room this evening, would you be in agreement with that?"

He watched her a moment, and the desire she read in his gaze made her heart thump hard. "I'll join you after everyone's abed."

She smiled and then screamed as he picked her up and threw her into the depths. She came up, and kicked further away from him as he chased after her. But her attempt to escape was short-lived, for he was too quick. Clasping her ankle, he wrenched her back toward him.

The action caused her to swallow a gulp of water and she coughed, trying to gain her breath.

He took her toward the shallows a little. "Are you alright, lass? I didna mean to drown you."

She chuckled. "You didn't drown me. I swallowed some water, that's all." She lay back into the water and floated for a bit. "Join me," she asked him.

He stepped over to stand beside her, and the touch of his finger circling one of her nipples made them pucker into hard nubs. "After tonight, we'll return here, and I'm going to make love to you on the bank of this river under the stars."

"Do you promise, Marcus? I'd hate to be let down by a gentleman not following through on his word."

She gasped as his mouth came down over one of her nipples and suckled it. "Aye, I promise, lass. This is one promise I'm not ever going to break."

CHAPTER 8

As Marcus bathed and dressed for dinner later that evening, then tied his cravat before the mirror in his room, he debated with himself over what he should do. How much to tell Henrietta before he slept with her? For tonight there was little doubt he would have her, in every which way he could and multiple times to boot if she would allow.

The idea of having her beneath him, of her calling his name while he pushed her toward release, had him hardening in his breeches. Picking up his glass of brandy, he drank it down in one swallow, needing to control his nerves and his desire.

The dinner gong sounded below and taking a fortifying breath, he left his room. He needed to tell Henrietta the truth about his boy. That his son was the bastard child to a woman who had up and left only days after giving birth to the boy. His shame was doubled by the fact that he'd taken comfort in the arms of a maid, working in his home and under his protection.

Some in Scotland had turned their backs on him due

to this truth, their religion and moral sensibilities not forgiving of his sin. Marcus did not care what anyone else thought, so long as his boy was happy and healthy, but Henrietta did deserve to know and to choose which path she would walk.

A slight pounding started behind his eyes with the knowledge of what he had to do.

He made his way down to dinner, thankfully not meeting either of Henrietta's family that had come to stay. The lass's mother wasn't someone he wanted to spar with too often. In all honesty, he was a little scared of the woman, but Henrietta's cousin Maggie was pleasant enough.

He came into the dining room to find everyone seated. Henrietta smiled when she caught his gaze. He smiled back in return. "Apologies for being late, Your Grace, my ladies. I seem to have a slight headache. Too much sun today perhaps."

Henrietta placed down her glass of wine and summoned a footman. "Have a tisane made for Lord Zetland, please, and bring it in here before serving him his first course."

The footman did as she bade, and thanking her, Marcus soon drank down the cloudy liquid and started on his turtle soup.

The courses came and went, along with conversations about the ton and what scandals were happening in London, including what Henrietta's brother—a twin no less, that Marcus had not known about—had been up to of late.

A couple of times Marcus caught Henrietta studying him, and with the pounding behind his eyes gaining strength, he hated the fact that he would disappoint her yet again by crying off their rendezvous.

"When do you intend to leave, Lord Zetland?" the duchess asked, slicing into her pork and placing a delicate piece into her mouth.

"I've been here a week already, so I shall not trespass too much longer on Lady Zetland. Winter will arrive soon enough in the Highlands and I'll need to be home preparing for the season before I'm snowed in and unable to leave."

Marcus met Henrietta's gaze and held it. What a wonderful week it had been. He could not remember a better time he'd had with a woman, or better company. Henrietta had been the perfect hostess, and just as knowledgeable as the steward who oversaw the everyday running of the estate. Marcus took a sip of his wine, admitting to himself that he would miss her.

"Is your home large, my lord?" Maggie asked him, seemingly genuinely interested.

"It's a castle, and overlooks Loch Ruthven. Of course it's in need of many repairs, but I'm hoping to have those completed within a year or two."

"It sounds lovely, my lord. I should like to see it one day," Henrietta said.

Marcus glanced up and didn't miss Henrietta's mother's curious expression at her daughter's words. Henrietta didn't seem to mind that her mother was looking at her. She simply kept looking at him, her beautiful blue orbs full of expectation and warmth.

"Talking of travel, Mama. There are still some details about Kewell Hall and the estate that I have to go over with Lord Zetland prior to my departure for Cranfield. It is probably best that you return to Papa in town and I shall send for you when I'm in need of assistance. Maggie can stay and keep me company until then."

The duchess wiped her mouth with her napkin, before

placing it back onto her lap. "I was meaning to speak to you about this, my dear. I had a letter from your father today wanting to know when I shall return. I think I will travel back to London, tomorrow even, and await your missive."

Marcus continued to eat, not wanting the duchess to see that her forthcoming departure left him relieved. Not that he didn't like Her Grace, but he did want more time with Henrietta, and with the duchess here, pushing Henrietta to leave for her own estate…well, that didn't tie in well with his plans.

"I should imagine a castle in the Highlands of Scotland would have to be haunted, Lord Zetland," Maggie said, grinning at him.

He chuckled. "If you ask my housekeeper she would say yes. But alas, I myself have never seen anything to cause alarm, and nor do I want to."

Henrietta sat back in her chair as the next course was served. "So your castle doesn't have any scandalous, dark, and hidden secrets that it wishes to hide? I thought all castles had some kind of mystery or story to tell."

Marcus choked on his wine and coughed, placing down his crystal glass. "No," he murmured, shaking his head. "There are no secrets at Morleigh Castle."

He turned back to his meal and concentrated on spooning a little bit of brown gravy over his pork. The claim that his home held no secrets was like weight of lead that lodged in his gut. He hated to lie to Henrietta, but he also wasn't sure what she would think if she knew the truth about him. That he had a son, a child out of wedlock, and not with a woman of noble blood, but a housemaid under his protection. It made him look like a vile cur, even though their relationship, as short as it was, was mutual.

A duke's daughter may not understand that he'd been

lonely, and his son's mother had offered herself first as his friend and then his lover. It was only after she'd thickened with his child that he came to know what a deceitful, money grabbing vulture she really was. She never wanted the boy, only her way out of servitude. Which he could not blame her for, but mayhap there were other ways to remove oneself from household employment.

HENRIETTA HAD BATHED after dinner and cheekily had ordered Lord Zetland one as well, but had asked the servants to send his in a little after ten. If her staff thought her illogical for doing so they would hardly say to her face, and with the knowledge that his lordship had a megrim, she'd used that excuse and asked the valet she'd assigned to him to pour a little lavender oil into the water to try to alleviate his pain.

With strict orders that the bath was to be cleared away the next day, she paced in her room before the unlit hearth and waited for the valet to be dismissed. Not that she'd taken up spying on her servants, but it was normally around this time that the staff finished their duties to the family and went downstairs to have their supper.

Footsteps and the unmistakable slam of the servant staircase door closing made her smile. Lord Zetland was alone. And possibly, right at this moment, naked in a bath.

The idea of seeing his toned, sun-kissed skin glistening in water again caused her nipples to tighten under her shift. She walked to the door and, opening it just a crack, looked out into the passage. No one lingered there, so pulling together all the determination and confidence she could, she started toward his room, making sure to close her own bedroom door before going.

She came to his door and with her hand paused over

the handle, a wave of nerves shot through her. Would he wish for her to come to him? Of course they had planned for Marcus to join her in her room tonight. But with his mentioning of having a headache, maybe tonight was no longer possible.

Dropping her hand to her side, she bit her lip in thought before the sound of Lord Zetland's voice inside his room made her start.

"Are you going to stand outside the door all night, Henrietta? If ye do not come in soon, the water will be cold."

She bit her lip, stifling a laugh, and entered, ensuring when she turned to shut the door that the lock slid home. Taking a deep breath she turned, and fought not to gape. He lay back in a bath before a small fire in the grate, just enough to take the chill out of the air.

Just as she remembered, his toned abdomen glistened with water, and he was at present rubbing soap against his skin in a manner that she would love him to do to her. The idea of feeling his work-roughened hands skim across her breasts made her ache between the legs and she swallowed a groan of need. It had been so long since she'd been with a man. Even before Walter's death.

"How did you know I was standing outside your door?" she asked, not moving.

He grinned, placing the soap on a chair that was beside the tub. "Some of the candles must be still burning in the passageway and I could see a shadow beneath the door. I took a guess it may be you."

"And if it hadn't been me?"

"Who else would it be?" he asked, raising his brow.

She had to concede his point. Shrugging, she stepped away from the door, slipping out of her dressing gown and letting it fall to the floor.

His eyes darkened and he paused from washing the soap off his body to watch her. "Are ye going to join me, lass? The water is still warm."

Oh yes, she was going to join him, but first she needed to take control of this situation. He was such a character, so confident, and a true rogue if she were honest. She needed to take back a little of his power and make him wrapped about her finger.

She looked down at her shift, saw her darkened nipples pushing against the fabric, and started to untie the ribbon that held the top of the gown closed. Untying it slowly, she met his gaze, then held it as she let her shift drop to the floor, leaving her as naked as a newborn babe.

In a flash he sat forward, taking her hand and pulling her to step into the bath with him. For a moment she stood before him, her mons at the height of his face. Stifling her mortification over that fact, she held her ground and didn't move.

"Do you like what you see, my lord?"

His hands ran up the back of her thighs, twisting inwards to tease her, so close to her core but not close enough. "Aye, I like what I see."

She moaned as he leaned forward and kissed her there, then took one of her legs and placed it on the side of the tub. His tongue flicked out, running along her core, kissing and laving her cunny in a way that she'd never known to be possible.

Certainly Walter had never touched her so. Their love-making had been sweet, and tender, but quick. Afterwards she'd always been left with a longing that was never sated. But right now, as Marcus kissed her in the most private of places as if he were kissing her lips, a little hint of what she'd been missing flickered within her body.

She spiked her fingers through his hair and his tongue

worked her, his lips suckling and kissing her, before slowly, and with so much care, he slid one finger within her core.

It was too much, all of it was more than she could bear, and with this unending torture pleasure rocked through her body, and she found herself grinding herself against his face, his name a breathless plea on her lips.

His other hand gripped her leg, and thankfully so, for without his support she would've collapsed into a heap upon his person.

With one final kiss against her mons he looked up at her, and the raw need etched on his face was enough to spike her desire for him all over again.

She sat, sitting astride his lap, and clasped his face. "I want you. I want you to take me. Now."

He growled, and lifting her a little, he guided himself into her. And for the first time in Henrietta's life, she was lost.

AT THE SIGHT of Henrietta in his room, all thoughts of his headache dissipated and Marcus's mind became occupied with more pleasurable musings. He had thought their dance into lovemaking would've been slower than what it was, but when Henrietta stood before him, a little unsure but full of unsated need, he'd not been able to stop himself from tasting her sweet nectar.

Just one lick and she'd opened for him, had accepted the pleasure he could give her and allowed him his way. She'd been sweet and wet, and having her grind herself against his mouth, well, he'd almost spilled his seed into the bath like a green lad.

Damn, she was beautiful.

Now Henrietta straddled his body, and with very little finesse he clasped his cock and guided himself into her tight, hot core. She shuddered in his arms and he kissed her deep and long, needing her to relax if she were to find their joining as pleasurable as his mouth on her cunny was.

He didn't force their joining, didn't clasp her hips and grind her atop him, as much as he wanted to. Instead, he simply kissed her, teased her into wanting more, and eventually, at an almost painfully slow pace, she moved, started to undulate atop him and take him fully into her body.

"Mmm," she breathed against his lips. "This is nice."

Nice… It was more than nice. Nice was a too tame a word for what they were doing, what he wanted to do. He wanted her with such a need that he physically had to stop himself from wrenching her from the bath, laying her atop the bed and taking her hard. Fast.

There would be more opportunities to make her scream his name in such a position, but tonight, in the warm soapy water, this location would have to do. "Blast, lass, you make me want you so much that even now, this isn't enough."

She increased her pace, and he couldn't help but reach around her, holding her hard against his chest. Her breasts rocked against him, their tight, hard beaded peaks rasping his chest with each movement.

He kissed his way down her neck, gliding his tongue along her collar bone. She was so small and delicate, her skin perfectly creamy with the slightest hint of blush marring her cheeks at their exertion. Tonight would never be enough for him. He wanted to taste her again, kiss her senseless more often than not, seduce her to be his, not just while he was in England, but forever.

She threw back her head and allowed him his way with her body, and for a moment he fucked her harder than he'd meant to, pushing up in her with fast, hard pumps that left him moaning her name as his balls hardened near release.

"Oh yes," she gasped, helping him to keep up the pace. She did not shy away from the rougher ride, if anything it heightened her pleasure which in turn made his double.

"Come for me, lass." As he continued his onslaught of their joining, water splashed onto the floor and he was heedless of the noise that they were making.

For the past two weeks they had danced around the attraction, and now, alone and together like this, that attraction burst into flame and they were both consumed. He wanted her to shatter in his arms, to take her pleasure, and he wanted to see her mouth open on a gasp as she peaked. He needed to see her eyes darken in enlightenment and enjoyment as tremor after tremor thrummed through her body.

She kissed him and he groaned as her core tightened to the point that he could not stop his own climax. They came, and he pumped hard into her wet heat, lost his self-control and his ability to think straight as his seed spent into her. All the while she rode him, took her pleasure, his name a whisper against his lips as she alternated between kissing him senseless and coming in his arms.

She slumped against his chest, her small kiss upon his neck making him feel things for this woman that he'd never felt for anyone before. He rubbed her back as they both caught their breath.

After a time, he clasped her face in his hands and made her look at him. He took in her beauty, that wasn't only on the outside. The woman in his arms had loved and lost, was a wonderful landlord and employer. A sensual, independent woman that he wanted. Needed for more than one night.

Her brightened eyes shone with newfound knowledge,

and he couldn't help but grin that she would be a woman to be reckoned with from this day on. There would be no holding her back from getting what she wanted. Hopefully him.

"You're so beautiful. I hope ye enjoyed our little rendezvous."

She smiled, and again his heart did a little flip. "I did. More than I ever thought possible. You brought pleasure to me twice, my lord. Is that common?"

He growled, the talk of what they had just done only ensuring that it would occur again, and soon. "Not always, but if you're sleeping with me, then yes. I like to give pleasure as much as I take it."

She studied him a moment, a little shadow crossing her eyes before she blinked, and it was gone. "Do you sleep with many women? I can only assume for you to say such a thing that this is a common occurrence for you."

He chuckled, shaking his head. "Nay, lass. Not common, but I'm no angel, dinna mistake me for one of those. I'm no virgin and I always set out to be pleasing in bed."

Henrietta looked away, biting her lip, and he waited to see what she would say. When she ventured no further conversation, he said, "Are ye jealous, lass?"

She shrugged, and for the longest moment she didn't do a thing. Then she met his gaze, trepidation in her blue orbs. "Maybe I am. I don't like to share, Lord Zetland. I usually get what I want, and I find that I want you." She slid against him and his cock, semi-hard but still within her, stirred at her movement. "While you're here at least. I want to enjoy our time together as much as possible before I return to my widowhood and you return to Scotland."

He didn't want to return to Scotland without her, and now he was determined more than ever to ensure that didn't happen. "We have some time before I depart, and now that your mama is leaving, we'll not have to be too careful about the estate."

"Maggie will still be here," Henrietta said, somehow clenching her core about him and making him lose his breath a moment.

He gasped. "Ah, lass. Do that again," he said, pulling her into a quick kiss.

She did and he moaned. "But I look forward to sneaking about, especially if it's you who is finding me."

And each time he did find her he'd have her, if she allowed. One taste and he was lost, and something told him that in this case, he never wanted to be found.

CHAPTER 9

The following morning Henrietta saw her mama off to London. Standing on the front gravelled drive of Kewell Hall, she waved until the carriage was out of sight.

Maggie, standing beside her, sighed. "Well, now that the duchess is gone, are you going to tell me why when I came to your room last night you were not there? In fact, I waited for you thinking you'd gone downstairs for a late-night snack or to get a book, but when you didn't come back, well, I had to wonder."

Heat rose on Henrietta's cheeks before she grinned. It was the most absurd reaction to such a question, but she could not help herself. When it came to Lord Zetland, she seemed to have the silliest reactions. Not to mention that after their bath last evening, she'd never look at the bath in the same way ever again.

"Do you really wish to know?" Henrietta asked, biting her lip.

Maggie's eyes widened with realization. "You slept with the marquess didn't you?"

Her friend pulled her to walk onto the path that circled

the house, and Henrietta went willingly. The fresh air may help her think straight. God knows after having Lord Zetland in his bed for the remainder of the night, she needed to gain her common sense back.

She nodded, wrapping her arm around Maggie's and smiling. "I did, cousin, and I must admit, it was more than I'd hoped for. He was so caring, so wonderful, in a way I've never known before. Even though mama did say sexual relations with one's husband could be so, I'd never experienced it myself."

"You found pleasure in his arms. Oh," Maggie said, a wistful look on her face. "How wonderful."

"It was the most wonderful thing that has ever happened in my life, other than my marriage to Walter of course." She sighed, recalling Marcus's touch, the reactions he brought forth in her body that even now, simply thinking about them, made her ache with need. "I'm going to be his lover while he's here. I want him, even now. I cannot stop thinking about him." The reactions she was having to this man were so unlike her. She'd not thought to look at another gentleman for the remainder of her life. But with Marcus, her steadfast resolve crumbled into ash. She simply could not stay away.

"Well," Maggie said, fanning herself mockingly. "You make me almost jealous. But know that I'm happy for you, Henrietta. I know you never do things so spontaneously, or without careful planning, so to take Lord Zetland to your bed must mean something."

Did it mean something? She certainly was attracted to the man, and perhaps because she knew she'd never fall pregnant by him, there really was little risk her reputation would ever be tarnished. As much as she would've loved not to be a widow, being one through no fault of her own meant she could take a lover, so long as she was discreet. A lot of women in the ton did so, and there was no bringing Walter back. God rest his soul, he was gone forever. Had been gone for a year now. When she'd received Lord Zetland into her library on the day of his arrival, she had not planned for them to end up so, as lovers and friends. But it would seem that fate had other ideas…

"I do like him. We seem to get along quite well, and he's caring and thoughtful. But do not read into our liaison any more than that. He's to return to Scotland and I shall eventually return to town. Our lives are vastly different, and he's not interested in staying south of the border. Not even for me." Not that Henrietta had asked him his wishes, but she did not want to overcomplicate their liaison. They were two adults enjoying each other, and nothing more.

"Have you asked him?" Maggie queried, looking at her.

"No," Henrietta said, "but I know he wishes to return to Scotland, and soon. He has a son to take care of and the castle is in need of repairs before the winter months. He cannot postpone his trip home just because there is someone willing to share his bed."

They turned around the corner of the home, and on the terrace Henrietta could see Lord Zetland sitting at an outside table that was shaded by a trellis with climbing roses over it. Also with him was the new maid that she'd hired, who was busy tidying away his breakfast dishes.

Beside her Maggie started talking about what she planned to do now that she was Henrietta's companion, and what Henrietta would allow her to do since they were cousins. Which was correct, for Henrietta would never order Maggie about or tell her she could or could not do something. They were like sisters more than cousins and Maggie deserved a happy and easy life, not one of servitude. She'd had enough of that when married to the earl.

Lord Zetland was looking over his paper at the maid, nodding every now and then, and even from where Henrietta stood she could see he looked a little bored as he listened to the young woman, who was speaking with great speed and gesturing hands. What on earth were they talking about?

The young woman spotted Henrietta and, bobbing a quick curtsy, headed indoors.

They walked the remainder of the way and Henrietta took a moment to admire his person. For the first time since Walter's death she had laughed, had fun, and had not been so concerned with the everyday running of the estate. Marcus made her remember that life was for the living and not to waste it by being cossetted away like a mourning recluse.

"I see you've met my new maid. Was she lost? The footmen usually serve the family."

Marcus stood and pulled out a chair for both Henrietta and Maggie. "She was lost, kept going on to me about the size of the home and how the layout of these estates are so different to the previous homes in Scotland she's worked in."

"Really?" Maggie said, looking up at the house. "Most houses of this size are all the same, I find."

"I believe she said she worked in smaller homes, my lady," he said, meeting Henrietta's eyes. "You look very beautiful today, Lady Zetland. You seem quite well rested."

Henrietta threw him a warning glance and Maggie looked at them with annoyance.

"I think I shall return inside. There is a new piece of music that your mama gave me that I want to learn."

"I will catch up with you directly," Henrietta said, turning her attention back to Marcus. "Behave, my lord," she said when Maggie had left. "You cannot speak with such openness even if my cousin is privy to our affair."

"She is?" he said sitting up and, as quick as a flash, leaning over and kissing her soundly. Her breath caught at the sensations his kisses, his touch, always brought forth in her and she clasped the lapels of his coat. "Did you tell her what I did to you last evening?"

Heat bloomed on Henrietta's cheeks and she pushed him away and back into his chair. "Not the details, you rogue, but I did tell her that I'd never in my life felt what you made me feel last evening. Even now, seated not three feet from you I find it too far away. I want you even now."

His lordship's eyes darkened with hunger and a shiver stole down her spine. The man could seduce her with one look, so it was only fair that she tease him in return. She found him attractive in every way, wanted him with a hunger that was never sated. Why should she hide her regard for him? During the time he'd been here they had become friends, and then that friendship had flittered into being lovers. She was a grown woman with needs, and if she wanted those needs met by the man seated beside her, then that is what she would declare.

There was no threat of them having a child, so the risk to her reputation was almost non-existent.

He reached out and ran a finger along her gloveless arm. "From the moment you left my room this morning I've thought of nothing but you. Tell me when I can kiss you once more."

She grinned. "You kissed me not two minutes ago. You cannot be so deprived."

"Oh no," he said, leaning forward to place his hand upon her leg, pulling it apart a little from her other. The action made her heart race and warmth pool between her thighs, but it was what he did next that left her breathless.

Thankfully the outdoor table had a long tablecloth over it, so anything they did behind the table was relatively masked from view. Lord Zetland reached down and placed his hand beneath her gown, running his touch up her leg, over her knee to slide up her thigh.

She placed her hand atop his on her thigh and stopped his course. "You cannot do that here, my lord. It is too precarious."

He shuffled his chair closer still and looked about. "There is no one to see."

Henrietta didn't venture to stop him again when his hand slid the remainder of the way, and touched her core through the slit in her pantalets. She clasped the table, spreading her legs further as he slid his touch against her mons until one finger slid within her.

She bit her lip and fought not to undulate on his hand. To do such a thing was not becoming or at all ladylike and yet she wanted to ride his hand, wanted his mouth where his fingers currently stroked.

"This is too much," she gasped, clasping his nape and forgetting that to anyone who could see that they would look awfully close. Lord Zetland leaned toward her, his hand beneath her skirts, his eyes burning with need and hunger. "You should stop," she begged, not meaning a word. She never wanted him to stop.

"But I will not, lass," he countered, his voice honeyed and brittle with need. "I want to see you, I need to see you shatter at my touch once again. 'Tis a sight that I will never tire of."

Henrietta moaned and throwing all decorum aside she kissed him, took his mouth with all the need that he evoked in her. He groaned and thrust his finger deeper, but slower, and the crest of pleasure that she sought curled more tightly within her but didn't peak.

He took her mouth without restraint and later Henrietta would curse the fact she had allowed such a public display of emotion. Such a public display of two people all but having coition before anyone who bothered to look outside.

"We should stop."

Marcus wrenched out of her hold and pulled her to stand, dragging her into the morning room just off the terrace. Thankfully the room was empty, but he did not stop, no, he continued on into the library where he shut the door, the snip of the lock loud in the empty space.

"Come here, marchioness," he said, his Scottish burr more accentuated with his desire. His chest rose and fell with each breath and she bit her lip in expectation of what was to come.

She edged back toward the settee, bumping into the table that sat behind it and ran the length of the chair.

"Perfect," he said, striding to her and hoisting her to sit atop it before he wrenched up the front of her skirts to pool at her waist. Henrietta all but thrummed with the expectation of what he was about to do. She'd never made love with a man on a table before, and her excitement doubled.

He ripped open his frontfalls, and his penis sprang to attention, thick and hard. She reached out and slid her finger along the silky, smooth shaft. He gasped, growling a little at her action.

Then he took himself in hand and rubbed the tip of his penis against her core, and she moaned, having no idea she could long for a man as much as she now did. How wonderful that women could enjoy a man in such a way. It was something that she could get used to and crave too often to count.

He clasped her hips and she watched, fascinated with

how he guided himself within her. Marcus met her eyes when he was fully sheathed and placed small, sweet kisses across her cheek. He moaned when she lifted her legs to sit about his hips.

In the bath last evening he had allowed her to pick the pace of their lovemaking. Allowed her to get used to his size, take her pleasure. But today, here and now, this was not the case.

His fingers dug into her hips as he thrust, hard and deep, his repetitive strokes causing her breath to catch. Her body was not her own, he owned her at present, and she threw her fisted hand against her mouth to stop herself from screaming his name as with one final thrust she spiralled into pleasure, her core thrumming and contracting against his ever-insistent phallus, before he too took his pleasure, her name a whispered rasp against her ear.

They stayed like that a moment, both lost within each other, before he said, "That, my lady, was not what I expected to do to you upon seeing you walking outdoors. But I must admit, I cannot regret having ye so."

She clutched at him, not wanting the moment to end as the final spirals of pleasure disappeared from her body. "I'm glad you did. It was most enjoyable."

He kissed her one more time, before pulling away from her and helping her to stand. He repaired his clothing and she watched as he tied his frontfalls back up. Something as simple as watching him now made her need of him spark to life. The idea that he would return to Scotland soon, back to his son and the duties as a new marquess and laird to his own tenants in the Highlands, left a pang of regret that he wouldn't be here anymore. It felt wonderful to have someone to laugh and converse with. How had she not realized how alone she'd felt after Walter's death?

Of course, one day he would remarry, have more children just as he should, and their time here at Kewell Hall would be nothing but a fleeting memory, a time of awakening—on her behalf at least—and a lovely rendezvous for his lordship while in England.

He tipped up her chin, a slight frown upon his brow. "What is wrong, lass? You dinna look very happy of a sudden."

She shook the depressing musing away and slid off the desk, righting her gown. "Nothing is wrong. I was merely woolgathering." She started toward the door, not welcoming the emotion that had caused a lump to form in her throat and unshed tears to blur her vision. "I'm going upstairs to freshen up and change for lunch. I'll see you directly."

MARCUS WATCHED Henrietta flee the library as if the hounds of Hell were after her. He allowed her space, but she wasn't quick enough to depart that he hadn't noticed her eyes had filled with tears. He too started for his room, and went over their interlude, every action he'd made, every move, kiss, and touch. Surely he'd not hurt her. He continued to his room and thought over what else could be bothering her.

Their lovemaking had been spontaneous. When he'd touched her leg out on the terrace he'd not meant for it to go as far as it did, or end up with them in the library making love with such passion, such unsated need that even now he wanted to be with her again. Even if to be simply near her, to talk and laugh as they did.

He sighed, walking over to the jug and bowl on a side table and pouring some water into the bowl to clean his face. He splashed water over his face, then using a cloth cleaned himself up as much as he could. Tonight he would go to Henrietta and ensure she was well, that she didn't regret their actions. He had never, and nor would he ever, force anyone to continue an affair if they did not want.

The more time he spent with the lass, the more he liked her. So much more than he thought he would when they'd tumbled into an liaison. He could see her beside him always, the stepmama to his son, mistress of both his Scottish estate and those in England.

He pulled off his cravat, laying it over a nearby chair. Henrietta had not hinted at marriage—she merely spoke about his impending departure as inevitable and with little emotional response. It did not make his reading of her easy. Did she wish to marry him?

He rubbed a hand over his jaw. For God knows he liked her, beyond any other woman before her, and forever seemed not long enough.

CHAPTER 10

After a quiet dinner, Henrietta retired to her room, and after a long, hot bath, Henrietta dismissed her maid and prepared herself for bed. She sat at her dressing table, brushing her hair, and wondered when Lord Zetland would leave. Tomorrow they were due to look over the crops to the north, and then return via the estate's flour mill. It was the last of the estate and the working farm that he'd not seen. After that, he would know exactly what he'd inherited, how it worked, who worked it, and what he earned from it each year.

With winter getting closer each day, he would probably leave within the week, and then her dalliance with him would be over.

She threw her hairbrush onto the table and started when her bedroom door opened and Lord Zetland entered quickly, locking the door behind him.

She met his reflection in the mirror and her stomach twisted into knots at the hunger in his eyes. How was it that he could look at a woman so, and even without words, tell her she was wanted, what he would do.

She licked her lips at the thought of having him in her bed, the delicious slide of his body against hers that she would miss terribly when he left.

"Bold, my lord. I did not know we had planned to be together this evening," she said, raising her brow.

He did not move, simply leaned against the door, a Scottish warrior out of a history book. And one she wanted to conquer.

"I came to wish you a good night, nothing more, lass."

She twisted on her dressing table chair, pulling the shawl about her shoulders. "Really? Merely a goodnight."

He pushed away from the door, and the muscles on his thighs caught her attention with each step he made. The buckskin breeches were really a very helpful article of clothing with being tight and allowing others to view all the assets that lay beneath.

He stopped before her, glancing down. "I've had ye today, lass. I'm not a beast. I will not push myself onto ye yet again."

Unable to resist, Henrietta reached out and laid her hand against his hip. He was so warm beneath her touch. Running her finger down the side seam of his breeches, she let her hand drop when she reached his knee. He stilled under her touch. He may say he would not have her again, but he did want her, and that truth filled her with a heady amount of control.

She stood, reaching up to wrap her hands about his neck. She kissed him, slow and deep, flicking out her tongue to mesh with his, and sighed when he gave way to his desire and wrenched her fully against him.

She went willingly, but slowly and deliberately pulled back before stepping out of his hold. "We have a big day tomorrow, my lord. You should probably get a good night's rest."

He studied her a moment and then nodded, willing to do as she bid, no matter that his breathing was as ragged as her own.

"Aye, of course. Goodnight, lass." He went to the door but paused before opening it. "This afternoon, you were upset. Please tell me you're not upset with me or what we're doing. Just say the word and we'll stop our liaison if that is the case."

There were many things wrong. One of which was how much she'd started to feel for the man who stood looking at her with such tenderness that it made her heart ache. But there wasn't any future for them, and if they were both to go on with their lives, forge new ones apart, she didn't need Marcus to form any feelings for her either.

She could not give him what he wanted. What all men of influence, titled gentlemen, needed for their names and great estates. She'd not been able to give her husband a child, and had they had the opportunity to be married longer, it would've only been a matter of time before Walter grew disappointed in her. Learned the truth that she was barren and unable to conceive. Marcus deserved to have more children, and as much as she'd love to give him another one, she could not and never would.

There was no future for them and so the constant bedding, the touches that left her yearning for more, the kisses and sweet words whispered in her ear, had to be lessened.

"There is nothing wrong, I'm merely tired, but I'll see you at breakfast. Goodnight, Marcus."

He frowned and looked as if he wished to say something further, but thinking better of it, nodded and left.

Henrietta slumped onto the chair before the hearth and sighed. What she was doing was for the best, for both of them. One day he would thank her, when he was surrounded by his children.

She smiled at the thought of it. He seemed to love his child very much, and the small boy deserved siblings. Henrietta adored having a brother, as much as her brother Henry revered having a sister. Marcus was a strong, capable, and moral man, perfect in all ways to bring up respectable, honorable children. Just how they all should be.

MARCUS LOOKED out over the newly turned fields and listened as the head farmhand talked of yields and what they were preparing to sow. As much as the information interested him, the woman who sat atop her mare, quiet and distracted, interested him more.

Something was up, and he'd be damned if he'd allow another night to go by not knowing what it was. Mayhap her monthly courses had arrived and that was why she pushed him away. But if so, being out on a horse for hours on end would not be the most comfortable for her, so he dismissed the idea.

No, she was fretting about something else and in turn, he was fretting about her.

"And how many bags per acre do you harvest?"

The farmhand went on with the information and Marcus half listened. He tried to catch Henrietta's eye, but she would not look at him. His stomach turned at the thought that she had tired of him, that when he'd taken her in the library the other day, his lack of restraint had disgusted her in some way. Mayhap she thought him a brute.

The farmhand stopped talking and, thanking him for the information, Marcus turned toward where they would head to next, the flour mill. "Lady Zetland, the mill I think. If you're ready?"

She looked at him as if surprised by the question, but nodding once, turned her mount and started east on the estate.

"The mill is quite large, I understand," he said, coming up beside her on his horse.

"Um, yes, that's right. One of the largest in Surrey, in fact. We produce flour for the surrounding counties."

Marcus was impressed. Looking ahead, he could see the pitched roof of a building along with the top of a breastshot wheel that turned as the water poured over it. "Do you have many men working the mill?"

"There are five men. I'll introduce you to them all once we arrive."

A clap of thunder above them startled his mount, and he cooed to his horse to settle him. Henrietta did the same to hers, but for a few steps it pranced with nervousness.

"There is a storm coming from behind us. We should make the mill before it hits," she said. It was more than she'd said to him all morning.

"We should pick up the pace, my lady, or I fear we'll not make it."

Pushing their mounts into a canter, they rode the rest of the way, but with the mill in sight, the first cold and heavy raindrop splashed against his cheek. They shared a look of understanding, and then the heavens opened above them.

By the time they arrived at the mill only minutes later they were drenched. The men who worked there were busy with their duties, and ensuring any wheat that was outside was moved out of the weather's way.

Henrietta introduced him, but said to the foreman that she would give Lord Zetland a tour of the mill. They started through the building, and walking behind her, Marcus couldn't help but admire the view—the sway of her hips beneath her sapphire riding habit and the straight line of her back.

"This is one of the mill stones in use here," she said, pointing it out to him. "Upstairs the grain is stored. We usually produce about 25 loads of wheat a week." As they continued the tour, the pride in her voice over the mill and how successful it was pleased him. It seemed this daughter of a duke enjoyed her duties, and all that she did as the Lady Zetland. "Are you pleased with your inheritance, my lord?"

She smiled up at him, and looking about to ensure they were alone, he pulled her into his arms. "Do you come with the inheritance, my lady?"

Her cheeks pinkened at his words and she grinned. "I'm afraid I do not. But I'm sure in time you'll still be pleased with what you have acquired."

He wanted her, so he doubted he'd be very pleased unless she stayed in his arms, forever. "And if I want more?"

She wiggled out of his hold and started off through a room that held stacked bags of grain. He followed and looked about as they came to an office with a large window overlooking the delivery yard below. The other wall sported a small fireplace. The desk had papers on it, along with a small bank of books on shelving behind.

"This is your office here at the mill. No one else is to come in here unless you're present. The foreman normally takes care of most day-to-day running of the place, but sometimes you're required to look over things. You can of course send your steward if you do not have the time."

"Did you work in here?" he asked, turning back from looking out into the yard. Henrietta sat at the desk, tidying up some of the notes that were before her. "I always did, because that's what Walter did prior to his death. We have a steward of course, but to be a good landlord one must know what's happening with one's own estate and people." She shrugged. "I simply continued in the same way."

"I shall ensure that all important things are brought to me for approval, even if I'm in Scotland. I shall not let down the people who rely on the produce of this estate, or those who earn their living working on it. That I promise ye, Henrietta."

"I'm glad," she said leaning back in her chair. "When do you think you'll leave? I'll work my own departure around the same time."

He sighed, coming to sit on the desk before her and crossing his arms. "I need to leave soon, under a fortnight I'm afraid. I have stayed longer than I intended as it is. There are some pressing matters in Scotland that I have to attend to, and I cannot be away from Arthur too much longer."

She didn't look at him, simply nodded. "Are you going to lease out Kewell Hall?"

"I will," he said, having decided to do that already. "But only when I know that whomever leases the property understands the importance of those who live here. Even so, I shall request monthly reports on the mill and farm to ensure everything is going as it should. I will not let you down, Henrietta."

She did look at him then, and the sadness in her blue orbs gave him pause. "I do not doubt you will be a good marquess."

"Henrietta," he said, reaching down and taking her hand. "Do you regret our dalliance? You are not your happy self, and I fear that I may have forced you into a situation that you did not want." Hell, he hoped that wasn't true, but he needed to know why she was so down-cast the last two days.

She stood and came to stand between his legs, wrapping her arms about his shoulders. "I've enjoyed our time together, but I'm sad that you're leaving. I think I shall miss you."

"You could always come with me." Marcus started at his own words before he thought over them and heartily agreed. He didn't want to leave any more than she did, it seemed, but his son needed him, and his Scottish estate was not in good working order such as those he'd inherited in England. He had to return home.

"I cannot come with you. For one, it would not be proper, and my life is here, in Surrey. I'm not ready for anything else at this time."

Did anything else mean husband? Well, he had two weeks to change her mind, and mayhap once he did leave, her longing and missing of him would have her arrive at his Scottish door one day soon.

"I understand, lass. But know the offer stands." And should she not come to Scotland, well, once the snow thawed on the highland ground, he would travel south again and win her hand and heart.

"Your son will be missing you, I should imagine. More so than I. It would be selfish of me to ask you to stay for a little time longer when you have so many other more important things to occupy your time."

Marcus took in her features, her perfect nose and wide almond-shaped eyes that had the longest lashes he'd ever seen. Her lips were supple, with the slightest hint of rouge upon them. His heart ached at the thought of leaving her behind. He wanted to tell her that she too had become important to him. That his time here in England had been one of the happiest and most enjoyable trips of his life.

"I had a letter from his nurse only yesterday, and he's been asking about the horses. I suppose when I return I shall start taking him out for rides, weather permitting. A Scottish lad is never too young to learn to ride."

"That is very true for English boys as well. My father also had me and my brother riding from the age of three. Only little ponies, you understand, but we're competent riders because of it."

Marcus pulled her closer, nuzzling her neck and breathing in the sweet scent of jasmine that permeated her skin. He could picture their own children learning to ride, of enjoying days out on the land, enjoying life together as a family. He kissed a little freckle that sat beneath her ear and she shifted her head to the side.

"Come to Scotland with me. I won't ask you for any promises, but spend winter in the Highlands with me, and after that, we'll see. Mayhap marriage with a Scottish lord will be to your liking after all." A future, children, and love…

He pulled back and caught her mouth in a searing kiss, taking all that he could from her while she remained in his arms. She did not pull away or deny him and a little flicker of hope sparked in his mind that she would think on his proposition.

She ran her fingers through his hair and pulled back. "I will consider your invitation, but I cannot promise any more than that."

"That's all I ask," he said, holding her tight and not wanting to let her go. Not now or ever. "Should we continue the tour?"

They'd been lucky no one had interrupted them or seen them, since neither of them had remembered to shut the door upon entering the room.

Henrietta pulled him away from the desk and, holding

his hand, dragged him out of the office. "Yes, there are a few more things I want you to see before we return to the hall, and I don't want to return too late just in case the rain decides to settle in."

The remainder of the afternoon went quickly, and just before they arrived home the heavens opened up and they were drenched yet again. Dropping the horses at the stable, they ran into the house, laughing at their unfortunate wet circumstances. Marcus loved the fact that this English beauty, a duke's daughter, was able to see the funny side of life, was not so serious and important to be lofty and aloof.

She was real, and a part of him warned him that he was getting too attached. Should she say no to coming to Scotland, he'd ask her to be his wife. He didn't wish to scare her away, but if she refused to come with no strings, perhaps if there was something tying them together then that would change her mind.

All that was left for him to do was wait and see what she would decide. He just prayed she would decide on him.

CHAPTER 11

Henrietta sat in the parlor that overlooked the terrace and sifted through the mail she'd received that morning. The morning light streamed into the room, and since the storm had passed them the previous night, she had opened up the doors to allow the cooling breeze to enter.

She picked up a letter from her mama, and read it quickly as it spoke of her brother, her father, and some of the latest improvements she was doing at the London Relief Society's Cheapside location.

There was a letter from her childhood friend who was traveling abroad at present, full of pleas for Henrietta to meet her in Spain. Henrietta looked out the open doors and contemplated it for all of a minute. Spain would be lovely, but Scotland was drawing her more if she were to go anywhere…

Since Marcus asked her yesterday about going back to the Highlands with him, her mind had been filled with little else. They had made love last night, and the tender way in which he took her, each kiss a promise, each touch heavily dosed with reverence, left her with little doubt that he was growing attached to her as she was to him. With each joining she couldn't help but feel her heart grow ever fonder of the possibility of a life together.

She put aside a letter for Lord Zetland that looked to have come from Scotland. There was one for her cousin Maggie, who had yet to wake up. She picked up her cup of tea and took a fortifying sip. As much as she wished she could go with him, throw caution to the wind and be his for a little while longer, it would not be fair for her to do such a thing. To give him hope where there was no hope to give.

She would have to tell him the truth as to why her decision would be no. To disappoint him would not be easy. The future he hinted at sounded perfect, but it would never come to pass. Not when she could not be everything that he wished.

He deserved to have children, to give his son a sibling.

"Good morning, Henrietta. I hope you slept well."

Henrietta started at her cousin's greeting and turned on the settee to smile at her. "Good morning, Maggie. Or should I say late morning, almost midday."

Maggie laughed and flopped onto a nearby chair, sighing in relief. "Oh, I'm positively famished. I've asked for my breakfast to be brought in here. I hope you don't mind."

Henrietta shook her head. "Of course not. In fact," she said, looking down beside her on the settee to find Maggie's letter, "this came in the post for you this morning." She handed her cousin the note, not missing the fear that crossed her visage when reading the address.

"Is it from the earl?" Henrietta asked, fairly certain it was.

"Yes. Probably another letter saying how much he

wants us to reconcile." Maggie met her gaze, and the fierce determination Henrietta read in her brown orbs was telling. Maggie meant what she said, and was steadfast in her decision. "The marriage was annulled, and I will never go back to him. He's brutal, and cruel."

"You're welcome to stay with me forever if you wish. You know I shall never turn you away."

"I know," Maggie said, reaching out to touch her arm. "And I'm thankful for it, for I'm not in any way looking to gain a husband ever again. One was quite enough."

"Talking of husbands…I need to confide in you about something, and I need you to give me your honest opinion."

"Of course," Maggie said, before thanking a footman who brought in a fresh pot of tea along with a plate of toast and fried eggs. Waiting for the footman to leave and close the door, Maggie said, "What is it you want to discuss?"

"You must promise not to tell a soul, ever." Henrietta threw her cousin a pointed glance and picking up a piece of toast, took a bite.

"I won't say anything," Maggie insisted. "Tell me before I expire of curiosity."

"Very well," Henrietta said, taking a fortifying breath. "The marquess has asked me to travel with him to Scotland. I think he is considering asking for my hand in marriage."

Maggie's eyes widened, before she jumped up from her chair and pulled Henrietta into a fierce hug. "Oh, my darling, I'm so happy for you. I have been watching the marquess this past week, and after talking to him numerous times, I can see that he's the loveliest of men. Warm and caring and I think possibly as nice as the late Lord Zetland."

Tears blurred Henrietta's eyes. "It isn't as simple as that, Maggie. I wish it was. But what I haven't told anyone —although my parents know of course—is that I'm unable to bear children."

"Pardon?" Maggie said, frowning. "What makes you think such a thing?"

"Because it's true. I never got my courses like other women. I've never bled at all. I thought that the doctor may be wrong, and I was so in love with Walter that I prayed they were wrong with their diagnosis. But not once in the year we were married did I fall pregnant. I sometimes think it was a blessing that Walter passed away so he never grew to know my shame. That I married him knowing the possibility that having children may never happen."

"Oh, Henrietta. I'm so sorry." Maggie clasped her hand. "And you think Lord Zetland will change his mind once he knows you cannot have children?"

Of course he would. A man of his status had to have heirs. His son would inherit, but what if something dreadful happened to him? Other children were always welcome with great families. She cringed at the unfeeling reasoning behind the choice. "Even if he does not change his mind, in time he may come to regret that choice and I will not enter another union without the truth being known. At the moment we're enjoying each other, and there are no rules. But if I go to Scotland, and the feelings he's evoking in me only grow, it'll be hard to not have a broken heart at the end of this affair. I cannot continue with this business knowing I'm barren and he wants children."

"Surely that is for him to decide. While I agree," Maggie continued, sitting back and picking up her cup of tea, "that the best thing for you to do is tell his lordship, he does have a son—an heir to the marquess title—already, so he may just surprise you and tell you that he is content. You're not the first nor the last to face this heartache."

Henrietta sniffed, thankful her cousin was here so she may discuss such matters. "You're always so forthright and honest. I suppose I'm scared that even if he's content now, he may not be in the years ahead."

"No one can know the future, but that is where I gauge the person's character, and if it's noble, kind and honest, then he will not lead you astray. Give you false hopes of a happy ever after when in truth, it is only a happy ever after for now, not five years from now."

"You make it sound so simple." Henrietta smiled, a little shimmer of hope lighting within her that maybe, just maybe, Marcus would not send her packing once he knew the truth. He was a good man, as Maggie said. Surely he would not lie to her and tell her what she wanted to hear, not what he wanted to say. "But you're right, I will give him the choice and we'll see. And I'll do it soon. He's leaving within a fortnight, so that gives me plenty of time to gather my courage and disclose my secret."

"I think that's best," Maggie said, nodding. "You'll see, cousin. He'll not be a disappointment to you."

Had not Marcus said the same thing to her only yesterday? She held onto his words and the hope it gave her and prayed he wouldn't fail her, or worse, break her heart.

CHAPTER 12

The following morning Marcus sat at breakfast and listened as Henrietta and Maggie discussed the latest scandal that the Duchess of Athelby had written to her daughter about. A debutante running off to Gretna wasn't in Marcus's eyes the worst thing—at least they intended to marry—but he absently smiled as Henrietta and Maggie seemed positively scandalized over the situation.

"Why are you grinning?" Henrietta asked him with a bemused gaze. "This is terrible. The Honourable Edith Feathers is throwing herself before a man with no fortune and therefore her parents have disowned her. What will they live on? She's only eighteen, and has no experience with the real world."

"Maybe he'll make something of himself and the lady's past fortune will not be missed. Not everyone marries for financial gain. I commend her choice. She was brave to follow her heart."

Maggie scoffed. "When they're living in flea-infested housing on the banks of the Thames I doubt very much that Edith will be thankful she followed her heart."

"You dinna know that is what will happen to them," he said, sipping his coffee.

Henrietta shook her head. "Their children will never be accepted into society. Even if they're married, they will be marred by speculation and tarnished by association. The children may even be termed bastards. Baron Feathers will certainly never accept them and therefore society will not either. How dreadful for the baroness to have her daughter do such a thing. One cannot recover from that."

Marcus narrowed his eyes, the mention of bastard children and the ostracising of them making his breakfast sour in his belly. "The English are too judgemental. The couple obviously love each other and should've been allowed to marry. That they married in Gretna ensures their children are not illegitimate. I should hope you, Lady Zetland, would be supportive of their plight."

She looked at him with something akin to shock and the thought of telling her that he had an illegitimate son left dread pooling in his gut. Would she be accepting of his boy? Would she cut anyone who talked down to or ridiculed the lad simply because of a situation not of his making?

"Well of course I would support her should I see her again, but it still does not change the fact that I think she's being very silly. The life Edith has been used to will be very different to the one that she will live going forward. I don't condemn her choice to marry a man she loves, but I fear she will find living conditions so very different that their love may not last under such circumstances."

Relief poured through Marcus like a balm and he released a breath he'd not known he was holding. "I can agree with that. She may find her life much changed, but mayhap in time the family will come around and enfold them back into their life."

"I hope you're right, my lord," Maggie said, taking a bite of her toast. "But if I know the Feathers at all, they will never forgive their daughter and they will make sure everyone she's ever known will follow their lead. I fear Edith's life will be hard."

"What is the boy's crime, as it were?" Marcus asked, curious. "Did he work? Or is he the penniless son of nobody knows who?"

"He was Baron Feathers' steward and was paying his way to becoming a minister with the church," Henrietta said. "He is not legitimate himself, hence why the family were so against the match."

Marcus had heard enough. Pushing back his chair, he walked from the room. He could not stand to listen to anyone talk down about a lad—even a respectable steward and a man of faith—and label him with such a derogatory term.

He walked to the library and, finding his own steward going over the books, he shut the door. "Malcolm, I need ye to find a gentleman who goes by the name of Mr. John Smith. He was working as the steward for Baron Feathers. The lad is also newly married to the Honourable Edith Feathers, and they've travelled to Gretna by all accounts. I want to finish paying for his studies in the church and have the living at Norbery House held for him until he's able to take up the position." If he could help but one man misjudged by society, then damn it, he would do it.

"Of course, my lord," Malcolm said, scrawling on a piece of parchment what Marcus was saying. "Is he expecting this offer, my lord?"

Marcus shook his head. "He is not, but they've been poorly treated in my estimation and they deserve better. Give him the offer and see if he accepts. I should think he will."

"Of course, my lord."

Marcus left the room, heading outside and toward the stables. He needed a hard ride to clear his head. To hear Henrietta speak so casually about a couple's downfall, and that of their children, didn't sit well with his conscience. Nor did it leave him with much hope that she would be accepting of Arthur.

And if she could not see past the fact his son was illegitimate, then there would be no future for them. No matter how much he feared he was falling for the lass. Or worse, how much he'd already fallen for her.

DINNER CAME and went and so too did nightfall and still Lord Zetland had not returned from his ride. Her maid busied herself getting Henrietta's room prepared for the night, but as she stood at the window, looking out over the grounds of Kewell Hall, the pit of her stomach churned that something was wrong. That something bad had happened to Marcus.

After leaving breakfast, she'd thought over their conversation that had made him react in such a way. The plight of Edith Feathers and Mr. Smith had hit a nerve with him, and she couldn't help but wonder why.

The sound of horse's hooves on gravel sounded below and she glanced out to see him finally returning to the hall. Where had he been all these hours, and why was he so upset over a little town gossip? She watched as he rode around the back of the house, then lost sight of him.

Dismissing her maid for the night, she grabbed her shawl and started downstairs. She met him in the hall that led to the back of the house. "You're back. I've been anxious about you."

He swayed and clasped the wall for support. "Ye have? Why?"

The smell of strong liquor permeated the air and his unfocused gaze and mussed hair hinted at what he had been doing all day. "Are you drunk, Lord Zetland?"

He chuckled and pushed past her, walking toward the foyer. She followed him as he made his way upstairs. At least if he fell down the staircase she could make some sort of effort to catch his sorry self.

"'Tis true, I am. Did ye know the Red Lion in Betchworth is well stocked of the finest Scottish whisky? I may have had a dram or two."

His words were slurred and a couple of times she thought she may have to try and catch him when his step faltered on the staircase. She took his arm when he made the first floor landing and helped him to his room.

His valet was waiting for him in his room, and Henrietta dismissed the man for the night so as to have Marcus alone. The older gentleman cast her a confused glance on his way out the door, before closing it quietly behind him.

Henrietta had not been in this suite since she'd walked in on him in the bath, and the idea of seeing him like that again had her cheeks heating. "Let me help you get into bed. You're quite drunk by the smell of you."

"Whereas you, my dear," he said, bending down and smelling her hair, taking a big gasping breath of it, "smell delicious."

"Well." Henrietta helped him to sit on the bed and started to untie his cravat. "Whether I smell delicious or not, I think it's best that you sleep off your little excursion today."

He nodded, seeming to understand, but all the while his eyes were glassy and unfocused. "What if I dinna want to sleep?" His hand reached out and clasped her hip.

Henrietta chuckled. "What do you want to do instead?" The moment she asked the question she regretted her words. Lord Zetland's gaze turned molten. His eyes, unfocused a moment ago, met hers and darkened with hunger.

"You."

Henrietta came back over to him, slipping his coat off his shoulders and unbuttoning his waistcoat. She could feel him watching her, and her blood beat fast in her veins at the thought of being with him again. Surely even drunk he may know what he was doing. And it wasn't like they'd not slept with each other before… She wouldn't be taking advantage of him…

"That is quite a forward statement, my lord. Do you think you're up to it?"

He took her hand away from untying his shirt and placed it on his groin. Henrietta's mouth dried at the feel of him, large and hard in his breeches. He was completely up to *it*, it would seem.

"Does that answer your question, my lady?" His attention snapped to her lips and Henrietta fought to calm her beating heart.

It certainly did. Even so, she wanted to tease him a little before she did anything. "You're drunk, my lord. You may be physically ready, but that does not mean you'll have the stamina."

He wrenched his shirt over his head and threw it on the floor. With him naked from the waist up, she cast her eyes over the corded muscles on his chest, the slight dusting of hair that ticked her breasts when they made love. Her hands itched to feel his warm skin. "I'll not disappoint ye, lass. Come here."

The deep, gravelly command made her sex ache. "You still have your breeches and boots on."

"And you're still dressed, but I can work with ye, even clothed such." He reached out to drag her closer and she let him, unable to deny him even herself.

His strong, capable hands slid up the back of her legs, lifting her gown before he found the hem of her pantalets. He slid them down, his hands leaving a trail of heat as he pushed her unmentionables to the floor.

She stepped out of them and kicked them away, before coming to stand before him again. "Now what?" she asked, hoping it was something wicked and naughty.

He reached under her gown again, and clasping her ass pulled her onto the bed to straddle him. He reached between them and flicked open his frontfalls, sighing when his member sprang free.

Wanting to feel him again, she reached down and stroked him. A bead of moisture sat on the tip of his manhood and she ran her thumb over it, watching his reaction cloud further with the want of her.

His breathing increased, yet he didn't look away from her, and the intense focus on her left her heady and alive.

"What are ye going to do now, Lady Zetland?" His voice was teasing.

What wouldn't she do would be a better question, after the numerous times they'd been together. The past weeks had been the most instructive and carefree of her life—certainly she hadn't known coupling could be so energetic or varied. Not to mention pleasurable.

She lifted herself up and, taking him in hand, lowered herself upon his phallus. He was large and felt even more so in this position, but where she thought there would be pain, she was only met with pleasure, and delectable fullness.

"God, Henrietta," he gasped, kissing her hard. "I canna get enough of you."

It was the same for Henrietta, and she rocked upon him, liking more and more this new position. "And I you," she said, meaning every word. To have Marcus leave, to not have him beside her at breakfast, or for a casual ride about the estate, not to mention in her bed, would be a severing she wasn't looking forward to.

He let her have her way with him, let her pick her own pace, and with that freedom the slow burn to climax was a torturous climb worth the wait. And then it burst within her. She called out his name as tremor after tremor radiated about her body, hard and fast, and somewhere in the chaos of her release she could no longer hold back the truth of her emotions. "I love you, Marcus," she gasped, kissing him.

He kissed her back, hard and deep, and flipped her onto her back, thrusting deep inside, shooting the last of her climax to peak in little tremors. "I love ye as well, lass. So much," he said as he found his own release.

His declaration made her vision blur, and he kissed away her tears before slumping to her side and pulling her into the crook of his arm. "Which leaves us with a problem, do you not think?" he asked, looking down and meeting her gaze.

"It does, doesn't it," Henrietta said, knowing that on the morrow she would have to tell Marcus the truth. Tell him that even though she loved him, loved him so much, she could not give him the future he wanted.

CHAPTER 13

Henrietta lay back in her bath and tried to ignore the fact that her maid was fussing about the room. The girl disappeared into her dressing room and Henrietta jumped in the bath when an almighty crash occurred.

"Is everything okay?" Henrietta called tentatively, wishing to be alone and to have some peace and quiet.

"Everything is well, my lady," her maid answered, before strolling back into the room with a handful of clothes. "I'll just take these downstairs to be laundered."

Henrietta nodded and sighed in relief when she was gone. Today she was determined to tell Lord Zetland the truth. What he did with that truth would be anyone's guess, but before they started any type of future together, they had to be honest. It had been a week since they had professed their love, and even though she'd planned on telling him the day after about her inability to have children, Henrietta had never found the right time.

But no more. Today she would do it. She washed herself quickly and got out, wanting to go downstairs and breakfast with Marcus. The past week had been day after

101

day of bliss, of dining together, picnics, and long horse rides about the estate. She'd not wanted it to end, and fear that he would not want her after he knew she would never bear his children had stopped her from confiding in him.

She shook the painful thought aside, not wanting to imagine such a thing—that Marcus could be capable of pushing her away. He was kind, loving. He would understand, she was sure of it.

She went into her dressing room and chose a light pink morning gown. Then she slipped on a pair of slippers and headed down stairs. Just as she hoped, Marcus was already at table, a large plate of bacon, poached eggs, and two muffins along with a steaming cup of coffee before him. He'd poured her a cup also, and she smiled at the sweet gesture. "Good morning," she said, dismissing the staff from the room and waiting for the door to close before she leaned over the table and kissed him.

He grinned back at her. "Good morning, lass. You look sweet enough to eat."

"Maybe later," she teased, smiling at his chuckle as she spooned some scrambled eggs onto her plate. They ate in silence for a time, before Henrietta said, "If you're free after breakfast, there is something that I'd like to discuss with you if you have time."

He searched her face, but nodded. "Aye, of course lass."

She smiled, and changed the subject to the weather and the possibility of them going for a ride this afternoon. If Marcus noticed her change of subject he didn't say, and she was thankful for it. Telling him the truth would be hard enough as it was, let alone trying to explain why she wanted to talk to him in private.

. . .

MARCUS WAITED in the chair across from Henrietta, who was sitting at her mahogany desk. He supposed the desk was really his now and he should be sitting where she was, but he liked seeing her there, in charge, lady of the house, strong and capable.

"You're nervous, lass. What is it you wanted to talk to me about?"

She fiddled with a paperweight, her long, delicate fingers shaking a little, and he reached over, stilling her hold. "Henrietta, tell me what's wrong."

She schooled her features. "There is something that I need to tell you. It's important and you ought to know before anything is decided between us regarding a future together."

An overwhelming sense of relief poured through him and he sat back in his chair. "I will admit that I'm happy to hear ye have something to tell me, lass, as I have also something that ye ought to know."

"Really? What is it that you wanted to tell me?"

He waved away her request. "You first," he argued. She had after all asked him to come into the library and discuss her matter, so it must be somewhat of importance.

"No, I insist." She settled back in her chair and watched him.

Marcus took a fortifying breath, hoping like hell she'd forgive him his actions. "You know I have a son, a fine, beautiful lad that I love and cherish." He frowned, the words harder than he thought to bring forth. "What ye don't know is that his start to life is not what one hopes for, and there will be repercussions for him for the remainder of his life. That my boy will face such censure is my fault and the blame lies with me." He should've told Henrietta the truth of his situation long before, and it shamed him that he had not.

"What are you trying to say?" she asked in a small voice.

"My son is illegitimate, Henrietta."

She recoiled from the news and Marcus winced. "Before I inherited the title of marquess, I had very little. The Scottish estate does not produce enough funds to keep Morleigh Castle running, let alone complete the repairs that I have planned. My estate is isolated and during the coldest winters becomes inaccessible. During one of these hard winters I sought the solace and company of a woman, a servant. She is the mother of my child."

Henrietta gasped, her mouth agape. "Tell me this isn't true, Marcus. You slept with your servant?"

Damn, hearing her state it aloud made it sound even more underhanded the more she stated it aloud, the more underhanded and seedy. "I was lonely, Henrietta, and I sought comfort in the arms of a willing woman. But if you're willing to accept Arthur, I know you'd be a wonderful mother for him and, God willing, to the children we'll have together."

She was silent a moment, and he cringed. What was she thinking? Did he disgust her now? "This happened a long time before I met you, and after the birth of Arthur, his mother wanted nothing to do with the babe even though I offered her marraige. She left and we've not seen or heard from her again." He leaned forward to take her hand and she recoiled further into her chair. "Please Henrietta, say something." Put him out of the hell he was currently living.

HENRIETTA FOUGHT FOR CALM. Marcus had had a child with his maid! Nor had he ever been married like she'd assumed since he was a father. All her dreams of them shattered like a glass mirror that had been dropped. Had Arthur been legitimate, she would've gladly been his mother, but with the boy illegitimate it changed things. Not that she cared either way if the child was born in or out of wedlock, but that she couldn't give Marcus any children that the law would allow to inherit his English estates. His title.

She sat for a moment, unable to fathom what she'd heard. She had come in here today to tell Marcus she could not give him children, never expecting to be told that he'd fathered an illegitimate child who could not inherit. Why had he not told her?

"How did you come to sleep with one of your maids? One that is under your protection?" She held his gaze and noted the shame that crossed his features.

"This is no excuse, but it had been a hard winter. No one had been able to leave the estate for weeks, and somewhere in between the cold days and even colder nights, I sought company. I know it was wrong, but it is in my past, lass. I want you to be my future."

The idea that his son was illegitimate settled on her shoulders like sack of flour. "You have no heir for the title of marquess."

He nodded once. "The Scottish estate will be his and I've already had a Will drawn up to state so. The English title and properties will be inherited by the eldest male child that I sire with my wife. I want that to be you, Henrietta."

Her stomach roiled at the truth of his words. If only she could give him one. She didn't care that the boy had a less than perfect start to life, but she did care that the situation now changed everything regarding what she hoped. If the boy was legitimate, there was a chance for them. If not, there was no hope.

She steeled herself, willing herself not to break down in a fit of tears. "I will speak frankly, and please let me finish before saying anything. The fact that you slept with your servant is distasteful and ill advised, but I do understand loneliness and what that can make someone do." *Such as fall in love with a man you cannot keep.* "As you said, your son, although born out of wedlock, will inherit the Scottish estates. But what of your English ones? Who will carry on the family tradition here? What will become of the people who work and live on the farms the estate owns if there is no lord to pay their wage?"

Marcus leaned forward in his chair. "We're young, Henrietta. I was hoping that you would marry me. That we could have children—an heir to take over the English title. I dinna wish to propose to ye when you're still angry with me—this is not how I imagined my proposal to be— but I love you. I want ye to be my wife. I want ye to be the mother of my children."

Tears pooled in her eyes and she swiped angrily at a tear that ran down her cheek. "I would like that too, but…" She shook her head, wishing she'd never started this affair that threatened to break her in two. "I'm unable to give you children, Marcus. There is no possibility, nothing I can take or do to change that fact. If you married me, your son Arthur would be the only child you would ever have."

He frowned, running a hand through his hair and leaving it on end. "But surely. You said yourself you'd only been married a year. Having children sometimes takes longer than that I think. You just need time."

She shook her head. "I don't need time. I've known this for a while now, and what I wanted to speak to you about today was this point. I was about to tell you the truth of my situation."

"But surely—"

"No, there is no 'but' in this case. I will not marry you knowing how much you want children. You deserve to have more, and I'm not going to be the one to stop you from doing that."

"We dinna have to have children, lass. I love you and you love me, surely that is enough."

Henrietta read the panic that flared in his eyes, hating that she was the one doing this to him. For all his past mistakes, he was a good man, and deserved only wonderful things to happen to him. He wanted more children, a brother or sister perhaps for Arthur. She had been wrong to allow their understanding to grow into so much more than sporadic tumbles into bed. Now both of them had their emotions engaged, and parting from him would not be easy.

"You mentioned at times your wish for more children. You not only need an heir, but you want one. It's quite clear to me that you're a caring and loving father. I will not deny you what you wish for most."

Marcus stood and came around the desk, pulling her to stand. He clasped her upper arms in a fierce hold, firm but not painful. "I want you more. Dinna send me away, not unless you're in the carriage right alongside me."

How he tempted her, but no. "You may say these things now, but in months to come, years even, you will grow to regret your choice and in doing so, regret me." She shook her head. "I will not be coming with you, Marcus, nor will I marry you." She reached out and ran her hand along his waistcoat. "Please do not make this any harder than it already is. Think of our time here with pleasure only. That is how I'll think in the months and years to come."

He stepped back as if she'd slapped him. "It's because

my son's illegitimate, isn't it? You dinna want to be associated with me because of the scandal that would be attached to our name should it become public what I'd done. We both know that in London, nothing stays a secret."

Henrietta gasped. "It has nothing to do with the circumstances surrounding the birth of your son. I do not care that he was born out of wedlock."

"You may not, but your family will, your friends. And dinna say that isn't so, for the letter from the duchess the other day about Edith Feathers running off with the family steward was proof of that."

"That is unfair. My decision has nothing to do with your son, and if that is what you think of me, you don't know me at all."

Marcus walked over to the unlit hearth and clasped the marble mantle. He sighed, shaking his head a little. "Mayhap 'tis best that I return home tomorrow instead of next week. If I cannot make ye change your mind, we cannot continue in the way that we have been."

Henrietta swallowed the lump that formed in her throat at his words. She didn't want him to go, not really. Even if it was for the best, to allow him to have a wife and more children, she wanted to be selfish. To tell him to stay. To bring his child to England and raise the boy here with them as a family. But she could not. She'd never thought only of herself, and she wouldn't start now. "I'll ensure the carriage is prepared for your departure." He looked over at her, and the pain etched on his features broke her in two. "I'm sorry, Marcus. I wish things could be different."

He nodded and strode for the door. "Aye, so do I."

CHAPTER 14

Six months later

Marcus had returned to Scotland determined to forget his few weeks in England in the bed of one of that country's most beautiful women. He thought it would be easy to forget Lady Zetland, to move on, but damn it all to hell, it was not.

Even with the knowledge that she wanted him to forget her. Had all but demanded he marry another and produce children by the dozen.

He shook his head and slammed the axe down hard on the fallen log just outside his keep. He could no sooner forget her than the Highlands could forget they were Scottish. She was in his blood, had wiggled her way under his skin, and damn it, he loved her.

Loved her wildly.

All that was left for him to do now was win her back. Prove to her that it didn't matter that he had no more children, for to have children with anyone else wasn't an option. He loved *her*. Wanted only *her*.

Couldn't the lass see that?

With winter coming to an end, just this week he'd had word that the roads were passable again, and so in the coming days he'd leave Morleigh Castle and travel to London. He would seek Henrietta out in town and see if he could convince her that she belonged with him. That she didn't belong alone simply because she wasn't able to bear children.

He wouldn't allow her to suffer such a fate. They deserved to be happy. Together.

HENRIETTA HAD RETURNED to town for the Season and regretted the choice immediately. Her mother, sensing her unhappiness, had thrown her into town events with such vigor that within the first week of being back in London, Henrietta was exhausted.

She stood beside her father at the De Veres' ball and watched the dancers partake in a minuet. Not that she really saw anyone at all, for her mind's eye only imagined someone else. Missing Lord Zetland so very much, she'd even a couple of times thought he'd been at a party or ball. The straight line of a gentleman's back, strong muscular shoulders, or hair that was of similar colouring and cut would catch her eye, and her heart would miss a beat.

But it was never him. She had herself to blame for that. She'd pushed him away, told him he'd be happier without her, and six months after Marcus had left Kewell Hall he'd not returned. So it would seem that her banishment of him had been what he wanted after all.

She shook the thought aside. This was for the best. He'd only gone because she'd forced him to, which she needed to do if he was ever to have more children. No one wanted a barren wife. No matter how wealthy or connected with the upper ten-thousand they were, at the end of it all, children ensured a family's survival.

"Father, I think I'll return home."

The duke turned to her, a frown marring his brow. "Let me find your mother and we'll come with you."

Henrietta lay her hand upon his sleeve, stalling him. "I'm perfectly capable of finding my way home, Papa. I'll send the carriage back for you."

"Are you alright, my dear?" he asked, always having a knack of sensing when one of his children were upset.

"Truly, I'm well. I'm just very tired."

Her father watched her for a moment before he said, "Your mother told me of Lord Zetland's visit to Kewell Hall, and that she thought you may have become close while he was there."

Close was not the term Henrietta would use. It was so much more than that. That her mama had picked up on the attraction, as new as it was when she was there, was telling. The pain of losing him, of letting him go, ate at her soul every day, and sometimes she wondered if the pain would ever ease.

She composed herself before she said, "We were close, Papa, but it was not to be."

He threw her a disbelieving look. Her father, even if he were a little grey about the edges, and had smile lines that were a little more pronounced, was still an attractive man for his age. And one of the best men she knew, even if he was her father and she was biased.

"Why was it not to be? I've remained quiet for some months, but I refuse to allow you to pine away and not live. This whole time you've been in London you've not had your heart here. And I think I know why."

Henrietta blinked back the tears that talking of Marcus

brought forth. "Why do you think that?" she asked, not willing to divulge her heartache just yet.

"You fell in love with him, did you not? When you returned to town it wasn't long before your mother and I figured out what was wrong." He took her hand and placed it on his arm, patting it a little. "Tell me, Henrietta, why Lord Zetland has returned to Scotland without you."

She sniffed, and swallowing hard wondered how she would get the words out without breaking down before the ton. "He has a child, Papa. One that was born out of wedlock."

"So?" the duke said, raising his brow. "I did not think we raised you to be so judgemental. Especially as we've had you working at the London Relief Society since you were a child."

Henrietta shook her head. "No, Papa, that's not it. I do not care about that. But his lordship wishes for more children. I could not allow him to go on believing there was a future for us, when there was not. He wants children. I cannot have them." A stray tear ran down her cheek and she dabbed at it with her gloved hand.

"Henrietta," her father said, placatingly. "Did I ever tell you why your mother and I never had any more children after you and Henry were born?"

"No, we just assumed you had all that you desired."

He smiled, patting her hand once again. "We did, never doubt that. We adore you and Henry, but we would've loved to have more children. But your mama almost died during childbirth, and the thought of losing her, the risk we would be taking should she be with child again, was not worth her life. And so we were grateful for what we did have. Two wonderful children, and each other. Having children is all very good, a wonderful gift, but people do survive, live full and rich lives, if they are unable or choose not to have them."

Henrietta had not known that about her parents. Looking across the ballroom floor she spied her mama, laughing with her good friend the Marchioness of Aaron. To have lost her mama, possibly never having her while they grew up, was a sadness she did not want to even contemplate. "But he wishes for children, Papa. I will not be the reason his wishes are not met."

"Was he in agreement with you? Was he happy and thankful that you told him to return to Scotland?"

"No," she said, thinking back on the day. "He argued the point with me."

"That's because he loves you, I think. You're present, alive now. A child, even if you did not have the medical issue you have, may never come. Sometimes that happens also. Women who are in perfect health can still be unable to conceive. But you, my dearest girl and flesh and blood, you're alive, in his life. Why would he not choose you over something that may never come to pass?"

The more her father spoke about her choice to send Marcus away the more she wondered if she'd done the right thing. Was he happy without her? Or did he miss her as much as she missed him?

"You think I made a mistake?" she asked, looking up at her father.

He smiled. "You were only doing what you thought was right. And even after all that I've told you, you may still hold to your choice. But I will tell you this, Henrietta. I love your mama. She is my life. The love of my life. And I would've forsaken the ducal line had I known we would never have children. She means more to me than a title. And if your Scotsman is as dejected, reserved, and pitiful as you have been these last few months, then I think you'll find that you are the love of his life. That you mean more to him than any title he may have inherited."

Henrietta bit her lip to stop it shaking. She had to go and see him. Find out once and for all if he regretted leaving or was thankful. Sitting in London any longer, feeling sorry and sad for herself, was not an option. "I have to go to Scotland."

Her father leaned down and kissed her cheek. "I think you do too, my dear."

Henrietta bade him goodnight and made her way into the entrance hall, where she asked for her shawl from the cloak room footman and ordered the Duke of Athelby's carriage.

The drive to her parents' London home was short. Henrietta alighted from the carriage full of eagerness to pack and be gone, just as a shadow stepped away from the home. She stifled a scream as a man in a dark redingote walked into the light afforded them from the street lamplight.

"Marcus?" she queried, and the driver, content that she knew the gentleman, drove off toward the mews.

"Yes, 'tis me," he said, coming to stand before her.

Her heart skipped a beat at seeing him again. She'd forgotten how tall he was, how much he reminded her of a Scottish warrior of old. "What are you doing in London?" she asked, not believing he was here, really before her, and not some figment of her pining, self-inflicted mind. She stopped herself from throwing herself at his head, begging him to love her just as she was, forever and a day.

"Is there someplace we can speak?" he asked, looking about.

"Of course," she said, realizing they were still standing on the street. She started up the steps. "Come into the parlor. I'll have tea sent in."

"Forget the tea. I just need to speak to you. Alone."

His tone, deep and with a brittle edge, was pleasure and pain all in one. Was what he had to speak to her about good or bad? Maybe he was here to tell her he loved her still. Or, the worst case, he was here to give her thanks, and tell her that he was to marry.

The idea left a sour taste in her mouth.

Without speaking, they walked to the parlor at the rear of the house, and Henrietta locked the door behind them to ensure privacy. They sat on a settee and, fighting the need to know right now what he wanted, she waited as patiently as she could for him to tell her his reasons for being in town.

He took in her features and gown with a look akin to adoration. "You look very beautiful this evening. Have ye been to a ball?"

She looked down at the golden embroidered gown with silk underlay, the diamond necklace about her neck. She nodded, keeping her gaze lowered so he would not see how much she'd missed him. How hearing his voice again was a balm to her aching soul. "I have, the De Veres' annual ball. When did you arrive in London?"

He threw her a sheepish look. "About an hour ago. I came straight here and have been waiting for you since the butler said the family were out for the evening. I took a chance and hoped you'd not stay out all night, but come home at a reasonable hour. Seems my luck is turning."

"So it would seem." She met his gaze and for a moment they just stared at one another. Her body thrummed with expectation, with wanting him as much as ever, and if he did not speak soon she would expire.

"I've missed ye, lass." He took her hand, kissing the inside of her wrist. "I should not have left Kewell Hall all those months ago. I should not have listened to you.

Instead, I should've demanded ye marry me. I dinna care that we'll not have children. I have a son, I'm perfectly content, I promise ye. But I'll only be perfectly *happy* if you'll be mine. Be my wife. Marry me, marchioness."

Her father's words floated through her mind and she blinked to clear her vision. "I should not have let you go and I'm sorry for pushing you away. I simply did not wish for you to miss out on what you wanted."

Marcus shifted closer to her, and as she caught the scent of sandalwood all was right in the world. "I'll only miss out if you send me away. I love you, Henrietta. I want to spend the rest of my life beside ye. I promise you nothing but joy. Just say yes."

She nodded and then chuckled as Marcus pulled her into a fierce hug. His strong arms and warmth enfolded her and she sighed in relief that he was here, that they would never be parted again. She hugged him back, never wanting to let go.

"We will be married in four weeks, and then we'll do whatever you wish," he said. "A trip abroad, a stay at your country house, or we could travel to Scotland where you'll see my beloved Highlands."

"I think first I need to meet your son."

"*Our son*, and if he loves you half as much as I do, you'll be adored."

Tears sprang to her eyes. She didn't think she'd ever cried so much since meeting Lord Zetland, but here she was, a sniffling watering pot. "I would love that. Please tell me you've brought him to London."

"I have, and he's at the Zetland townhouse." He tipped up her chin and feathered her lips, her chin and cheeks with kisses. "Stay with me tonight and meet our son tomorrow. I dinna want to be parted from ye again."

Henrietta stood, pulling him to stand. "Let me get my

shawl and we'll leave directly," she said, laughing at the wicked determination that entered his eyes. For the first time in months she felt alive again, her mind clear, unworried, and her heart filled with joy.

Her Scotsman followed her and soon they were ensconced in the marquess's carriage. The night was filled with joy, and wickedness, and everything she'd ever hoped for. And the following morning, Henrietta met her child.

EPILOGUE

Twelve years later

Henrietta sat atop her mount on the side of the Scottish mountain range that overlooked Loch Ruthven and watched as her son, Arthur, crawled along the ground trying to get a better vantage point to shoot the deer that was just over the ridge.

"How is he doing?" Marcus whispered, coming to stand beside her, his horse's reins loose in his hands.

"I think he has one in his sight. He's become very quiet and still." Henrietta looked down at Marcus, the love she had for the man standing at her feet having never lessened over the years they'd been married. If anything, it had only grown.

He'd kept to his promise—had loved her wildly, devoted his every spare minute to ensuring she was happy, and cared for her and Arthur with a ferocity that was unmatched. He was truly the best of men, and even though they'd never had any children of their own, Henrietta never felt as though she'd missed out.

Marcus's son—her son—meant the world to them, and she was so proud of the young man he was growing into.

A shot rang out and Arthur lifted his head to look above the gun's scope. He turned toward them, a large smile across his handsome features. "A clean shot, Mama."

Henrietta sighed, smiling with pride at her boy. "Well done, Arthur."

Marcus clasped her thigh, rubbing it a little. "Have I told ye today how bonny you look up on that horse, the Highlands behind you, your hair askew, and your cheeks pinkened with cold?"

She chuckled, pushing at his hand. "You, sir, are no gentleman. I look like a fright."

"And you love me for that," he said, winking at her.

She leaned down, clasping his kilt that he had thrown up over one shoulder for extra warmth, and pulling him in for a kiss. "Aye, I do love you, don't I," she said, in the best Scottish brogue she could muster. "And I always will."

He reached up and pulled her off the horse. She laughed before he took her lips and kissed her with such passion that she was left breathless. The sound of their son complaining about them met her ears and she smiled.

Marcus grinned. "And I love you, lass. Always and forever." *My love...*

Dear Reader,

Thank you for taking the time to read *To Marry a Marchioness*! I hope you enjoyed the sixth book in my Lords of London series.

I'm forever grateful to my readers, so if you're able, I would appreciate an honest review of *To Marry a Marchioness*. As they say, feed an author, leave a review! You can contact me at tamaragillauthor@gmail.com or sign up to my newsletter to keep up with my writing news.

If you'd like to learn about book one in my League of Unweddable Gentlemen series, *Tempt Me, Your Grace*, please read on. I have included the prologue for your reading pleasure.

Tamara Gill

TEMPT ME, YOUR GRACE

League of Unweddable Gentlemen, Book 1

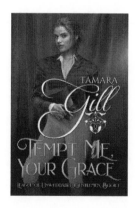

She was banished from England…and she banished him from her heart.

Upon her return to England following her father's death, Miss Ava Knight becomes the owner of one of the largest racehorse estates in the country. There's only one problem: the future of the estate requires a strong breeding program with the services of a stallion named, Titan. A shame that the horse is owned by a man she swore to never see again.

The Duke of Whitstone, Tate Wells, was heartbroken when Ava abandoned him on the night of their elopement, and he vowed to never lay eyes on Ava again. Despite Tate's unwillingness to forgive Ava, she comes to his aid during a deliberately lit fire at his estate. Someone is determined to destroy them. Now, the two are forced to work together to ensure the safety of their horses and their homes.

Will their previous feelings for each other rekindle their love, or will their feelings stall out at the starting gates?

PROLOGUE

Knight Stables, Berkshire, 1816

Miss Avelina Knight, Ava to those close to her, tightened the girth of her mount, and checked that the saddle wouldn't slip whilst hoisting herself onto one stirrup. With a single candle burning in the sconce on the stables' wall, she worked as quickly and as noiselessly as she could in the hopes that the stable hands that slept in the lofts above wouldn't wake.

Pleased that the saddle would hold, and that her mount was well watered before her departure, she walked Manny out of the stables as silently as possible, cringing when the horse's shod feet made a clip clop sound with each step.

Ava blew out the candle as she walked past it, and picking up her small bag, threw it over her horse's neck before hoisting herself up into the saddle. She sat there a minute, listening for any noise, or the possibility that someone was watching. Happy that everything remained quiet, she nudged her mount and started for the eastern gate.

There was still time and she didn't need to rush, now that she was on her way. Tate had said he'd meet her at their favorite tree at three in the morning, and it was only half past two.

She pushed Manny into a canter, winding her way through several horse yards that surrounded her home and past the gallop her father used to train their racing stock. Or what was once her home. From tonight onward, her life would finally begin. With Tate, she would travel the world, make love under the stars if they so wished, and not have to be slaves to either of their families' whims or Society and its strictures.

Tate and she would find a new life. A new beginning. Just the two of them until they expanded their family to add children in a few years.

Pleasure warmed her heart at the knowledge, and she couldn't stop the soft laugh of delight which escaped her.

In time, Ava hoped her father would forgive her, and maybe when they returned, happily married with children even, her father would be pleased.

The shadowy figure of a man stood beneath the tree. Yet from the stance and girth of the gentleman, it did not look like Tate. Coldness swept over her skin, and she narrowed her eyes, trying to make out who was waiting for her. Her stomach in knots, she pushed her horse forward unsure what this new development meant.

Ava looked about, but could see no one else. With a couple of more steps she gasped when she finally made out the ghostly form. Her father.

Her heart pounded a frantic beat. How was it he was here and not Tate? They had been so careful, so discreet. Why, they had not even circulated within the same social sphere to be heard whispering or planning. With Tate being the heir to his father, the Duke of Whitstone and

Ava only the daughter of a racehorse notable, their lives couldn't be more different.

Ava rode her horse up to the tree. She saw little point in turning back.

Pulling up before her father, she met his gaze, as much of it as she could make out under the moonlit night.

"Ava, climb down, I wish to speak to you."

His tone was not angry, but guarded, and the pit of her stomach lurched at the notion that something dreadful had happened to Tate. Had he been hurt? Why wasn't he here to meet her instead?

She jumped down, walking up to him, her mount following on her heels.

"Papa, what are you doing here?" she asked, needing to know and knowing there was little point in ignoring the fact that he'd found her out.

She dropped her horse's reins, and her mount reached down to nibble on the grass.

Her father's face took on a stern cast. "The Marquess of Cleremore will not be meeting you here, Ava. I received a note late last night notifying me that, as we speak, his lordship has been sent to London to catch the first boat out to New York. From what his father, the Duke of Whitstone, states, this was the marquess' decision. Tate confided in his father the predicament he'd found himself in with you, and that he didn't know how to untangle himself from having to marry a woman who was not his equal."

Ava stared at her father, unable to fathom what he was saying. Hollowness opened up in her chest and she clasped her shawl as if to halt its progress. Tate had left her? No, it couldn't be true. "But that doesn't make any sense, Papa. Tate loves me. He said so himself at this very spot." Surely she couldn't have been wrong about his affections. People did not declare such emotions unless they were true. She certainly had not.

She loved Tate. Ava thought back to all the times he'd taken liberties with her, kissing her, touching her, spending copious amounts of time with her and it had all been meaningless to him. She had been a mere distraction, a plaything for a man of his stature.

Her stomach roiled at the idea and she stumbled to the tree, clutching it for support. "No. I do not believe it. Tate wouldn't do that to me. He loves me as I love him and we're going to marry each other." Ava stared down at the ground for a moment, her mind reeling before she rounded on her father. "I need to see him. He needs to tell me this to my face."

"Lord Cleremore has already left for town. And by morning, he'll be on a ship to America." Her father sighed, coming over to her and taking her hand. "I thought your attachment to him was a passing folly. His lordship was never for you, my dear. We train and breed racehorses and, in England, people like us do not marry future dukes."

Ava stared at her father, not believing this was happening. She'd thought tonight would be the start of forever, but it was now the beginning of the end. Her eyes smarted and she was powerless to hold onto her composure. "But I love him," she whispered, her voice cracking.

Her father, a proud but humble man from even humbler beginnings, straightened his spine. "I know you think you did, but it wasn't love. You're young, too young to be throwing your life away on a boy who would have his way with you and then marry another titled, well-connected woman."

"I'm not ruined or touched, father. Please don't speak in such a way." She didn't want to imagine that Tate could treat her with so little respect, but what her father said was worth thinking over. The past few weeks with Tate had left very little room other than to plan, to plot. Would they have thought differently, would Tate have acted differently if he'd been older, more mature? If his departure showed anything, it was certainly that what her father was saying was true. He had regretted his choice and had left instead of facing her. Letting her down as a gentleman should, had not been his course. It showed how little he thought of her and the love she'd so ardently declared to him.

She swiped at her cheeks, wanting to scream into the night at the unfairness of it all.

"I'm sorry," she said, looking at her half boots and not able to meet his gaze. *How could he have done this to me?* She would never forgive him.

He sighed. "There is one more thing, my dear."

More! What else could there possibly be to say! "What, papa?" she asked, dread formed like a knot in her stomach at her father's ashen countenance. She'd seen a similar look from him when he'd come to tell her of her mother's passing and it was a visage she'd never wanted to see again. Ava clutched the tree harder.

"I'm sending you away to finishing school in France. I've enrolled you at Madame. Dufour's Refining School for Girls. It's located in southern France. It comes highly recommended and will help prepare you for what's to come in your life; namely, running Knight Stables, taking over from me when the time comes."

Finishing school! "You're sending me to France! But Papa, I don't need finishing school. You know that I'm more than capable of taking over the running of the stables already. And I know my manners, how to act in both upper- and lower-class society. Please do not send me away. I won't survive without you and our horses. Don't take that away from me, too." *Not when I've already lost the happiness of which I was so certain.*

He shushed her, pulling her into his arms. Ava shoved him away, pacing before him.

Her father held out his hand, trying to pacify her. "You'll thank me one day. Trust me when I tell you, this is a good thing for you, and I'll not be moved on my decision. We're leaving for Dover tomorrow and I, myself, will accompany you to ensure your safe arrival."

"What." She stopped pacing. "Father, please don't do this. I promise not to do such a silly, foolish thing again. You said yourself Tate was leaving. There is no reason to send me away as well." Just saying such a thing aloud hurt and Ava clutched her stomach. To have loved and lost Tate would be hard enough; nevertheless being sent away to a foreign country, alone and without any friends or support was too much to bear.

He came over to her, pulling her against him and kissing her hair. "This is a good opportunity for you, Ava. I have worked hard, saved, and invested to enable me to give you all that a titled child could receive. I want this for you. Lord Cleremore may not think that you're suitable for him, but we shall prove him wrong. Make me proud, use the education to better yourself, and come home. Promise me you will do so."

Ava slumped against him. Her father had never been flexible on things and once he'd made a decision it was final. There was no choice; she would have to do as he said. "I will go as I see there is little I can say to change your mind."

"That's my girl." He pulled back and whistled for her mount.

She couldn't even manage a half-smile as Manny trotted over to them.

"Let us go. I'm sure by the time we arrive back home breakfast will not be far away."

Using a nearby log, Ava hoisted herself up onto the saddle. The horse, as if knowing her way home, started ambling down the hill. Light shone in the eastern sky and glancing to her left, Ava watched the sun rise over her land. Observed the dawn of a new day, marking a new future even for her, one that did not include Tate, Marquess Cleremore and future Duke of Whitstone.

A lone tear slid down her cheek and she promised herself, there and then, never to cry over Tate again or any other man. She'd given him her heart and trust and he had callously broken them. That the tear drying on her cheek would be the last she ever afforded him.

And his precious dukedom that he loved so dearly. More dearly than her.

KISS THE WALLFLOWER SERIES
AVAILABLE NOW!

If the roguish Lords of London are not for you and wall-flowers are more your cup of tea, then below is the series for you. My Kiss the Wallflower series are linked through friendship and family in this four-book series. You can grab a copy on Amazon or read free through KindleUnlimited.

LEAGUE OF UNWEDDABLE GENTLEMEN SERIES AVAILABLE NOW!

Fall into my latest series, where the heroines have to fight for what they want, both regarding their life and love. And where the heroes may be unweddable to begin with, that is until they meet the women who'll change their fate. The League of Unweddable Gentlemen series is available now!

ALSO BY TAMARA GILL

Wicked Widows Series

TO DREAM OF YOU

League of Unweddable Gentlemen Series

TEMPT ME, YOUR GRACE

HELLION AT HEART

DARE TO BE SCANDALOUS

TO BE WICKED WITH YOU

KISS ME DUKE

Kiss the Wallflower series

A MIDSUMMER KISS

A KISS AT MISTLETOE

A KISS IN SPRING

TO FALL FOR A KISS

KISS THE WALLFLOWER - BOOKS 1-3 BUNDLE

Lords of London Series

TO BEDEVIL A DUKE

TO MADDEN A MARQUESS

TO TEMPT AN EARL

TO VEX A VISCOUNT

TO DARE A DUCHESS

TO MARRY A MARCHIONESS

LORDS OF LONDON - BOOKS 1-3 BUNDLE

LORDS OF LONDON - BOOKS 4-6 BUNDLE

To Marry a Rogue Series
ONLY AN EARL WILL DO
ONLY A DUKE WILL DO
ONLY A VISCOUNT WILL DO

A Time Traveler's Highland Love Series
TO CONQUER A SCOT
TO SAVE A SAVAGE SCOT

Time Travel Romance
DEFIANT SURRENDER
A STOLEN SEASON

Scandalous London Series
A GENTLEMAN'S PROMISE
A CAPTAIN'S ORDER
A MARRIAGE MADE IN MAYFAIR
SCANDALOUS LONDON - BOOKS 1-3 BUNDLE

High Seas & High Stakes Series
HIS LADY SMUGGLER
HER GENTLEMAN PIRATE
HIGH SEAS & HIGH STAKES - BOOKS 1-2 BUNDLE

Daughters Of The Gods Series
BANISHED-GUARDIAN-FALLEN
DAUGHTERS OF THE GODS - BOOKS 1-3 BUNDLE

Stand Alone Books

TO SIN WITH SCANDAL

OUTLAWS

ABOUT THE AUTHOR

Tamara is an Australian author who grew up in an old mining town in country South Australia, where her love of history was founded. So much so, she made her darling husband travel to the UK for their honeymoon, where she dragged him from one historical monument and castle to another.

A mother of three, her two little gentlemen in the making, a future lady (she hopes) and a part-time job keep her busy in the real world, but whenever she gets a moment's peace she loves to write romance novels in an array of genres, including regency, medieval and time travel.

www.tamaragill.com
tamaragillauthor@gmail.com

Printed in Germany
by Amazon Distribution
GmbH, Leipzig